D0718482

SHOE FLY BABY

SHOE FLY BABY

The Asham Award Short Story Collection

Edited by Kate Pullinger

BLOOMSBURY

First published 2004

Selection copyright © 2004 by The Asham Trust
Foreword copyright © Carole Buchan

The copyright of the individual stories remains with the respective authors

The moral right of the authors has been asserted

Bloomsbury Publishing Plc, 38 Soho Square, London W1D 3HB

A CIP catalogue record is available from the British Library

ISBN 0 7475 6686 0

10 9 8 7 6 5 4 3 2 1

Typeset by Hewer Text Ltd, Edinburgh
Printed in Great Britain by Clays Ltd, St Ives plc

All papers used by Bloomsbury Publishing are natural,
recyclable products made from wood grown in
well-managed forests. The manufacturing processes
conform to the environmental regulations of the
country of origin.

www.bloomsbury.com/asham

CONTENTS

CAROLE BUCHAN

Foreword

A SHAM HOUSE in Sussex, once home to Virginia Woolf, was demolished a decade ago, but its name has been the inspiration for hundreds of women writers in the eight years since the Asham Award was first launched.

The Asham Literary Endowment Trust was set up to support and encourage new writers. The Asham Award celebrates women's writing in particular, and Woolf's passionate stance – as set out in her book *A Room of One's Own* – that women need support and resources to be creative, is as relevant today, despite legislation and a philosophy of equality, as it was seventy years ago.

Women today may have the freedom which Woolf's generation fought for, but it is freedom at a price. Many are juggling a demanding career with home, partner and children, while others lack the confidence to strike out on their own, fearing rejection and criticism. The Asham Award seeks to encourage and to offer unknown women writers the opportunity to have their work published alongside that of established authors. Many of our most distinguished contemporary writers have contributed to the Asham anthology over the years, and we are grateful to them and to Kate Pullinger, who edits this latest collection and who has helped each of our winning writers to prepare her story for publication.

We are indebted to Bloomsbury for its support and belief in the work of the Asham Trust and for giving twelve new writers the opportunity of seeing their stories in print, alongside those of Lesley Glaister, Liz Jensen, Maggie O'Farrell, Kamila Shamsie, Francine Stock and Erica Wagner. The links between Asham and Bloombury Publishing are particularly significant, for Bloomsbury is an area of London closely associated with Woolf and a generation of trailblazing writers and artists.

We are grateful also to Viridor, who sponsored this year's Award, and who own the site where Asham House once stood.

The Asham Trust believes strongly in the importance of the short story in today's world. It has immediacy and impact, yet has its roots in the past, where some of our greatest writers – many of them women – perfected the art of the short story. We are delighted that greater prominence is being given to this artform today and that a tradition so important in our literary heritage is enjoying a revival in the new millennium.

This collection celebrates both the diversity of the short story and of women's writing. We hope you find these stories challenging, exciting and thought-provoking.

Carole Buchan,
Asham Literary Endowment Trust,
Lewes, East Sussex.

THE ASHAM AWARD 2003

First Prize   *Shoe Fly Baby* by Victoria Briggs

Second Prize   *The Monarch* by Lucy Lepchani

Joint Third Prize   *Victoria* by Hilary Plews
                        Gravity by Naomi Alderman

RACHAEL MCGILL

Butter Fish Parrot Fish

I'VE GOT a baby daughter and I take her to the pub. I put her in one of those harnesses in front of me. Her name's Pearl. My brother says: 'That's a bloody good pulling technique. That's the best pulling technique I've ever heard of.'

I do get plenty of attention from women. They really go for the name Pearl. I like it cause it's my daughter's name now, it's her. But I don't know why we chose it. I reckon my wife chose it. My wife thought a baby might be like a little jewel. Get it out on special occasions and polish it.

My wife didn't like mess. It seems to me that there were big bits missing from her. Maybe there are big bits missing from everyone.

I like meeting women in pubs. Women talk. They'll say all sorts of stuff. There's a girl I see in the pub, red hair, Lorraine. She said to me: 'I don't remember the first or the last time I made love to anyone.' Debbie the barmaid says 'People have no idea how to ask for each other.'

I like meeting women in pubs. Because of Pearl they don't think I want sex. I like the way they smile at me. They think I must be some kind of saint because my wife left me with a baby and I'm bringing her up on my own and taking her to the pub. I don't see that I've got any choice.

Women are very practical. If they want to walk away they walk away. Women are much more practical than men.

'Men will sit in a dirty room smoking for weeks,' Debbie says. 'They will sit in the rain at bus stops believing they're performing extreme acts for love.' I'm sure we all like to sit in the rain at bus stops pretending we're performing extreme acts for love.

I think about my wife every minute of the day. She said 'Do you think I just want to have my cake and eat it?' I said, 'I think you want to have all the cake in the world and eat it.'

'And so she should,' said the old lady in the laundrette. 'She has the teeth.'

My wife will get all the cake in the world and eat it without me and without her daughter and she'll be happy. I don't pretend to the women in pubs that I'm happy. That's why I always go home on my own.

Lorraine says, 'Happiness is irrelevant if you ask me.' Embrace the loneliness, I'm saying to myself, let it in. Embrace the fucking loneliness.

The news says: 'Turtles Killed.'

'Girl, eight, loses her foot in bomb terror.'

After a while we have to go home anyway because Pearl doesn't like the smoke.

The fishmonger says 'Butter Fish Parrot Fish.'

I always have dreams. I dream that Pearl is hurt and it's my fault. I dream that I open the bathroom door and all my wife's ex-lovers come out wearing their pyjamas. I dream that my wife is trying to phone me but I never get the message.

'This is BT Callminder. You have one new message.'

'This is BT Callminder. The same person phoned again and you weren't here.'

'This is BT Callminder. The same person phoned again. She didn't leave a message but she was very sad.'

I'm bonding with my own insanity. Hah.

The billboard says, 'You can't have flu. The office needs you.'

The old lady in the laundrette says Mrs Oldingham died of the flu. She didn't have the jab because she didn't like the lady doctor.

I said to my wife: 'You're my favourite thing in the twentieth and the twenty-first centuries.'

She said, 'One day you'll find out I'm selfish.'

I said, 'One day you'll find out I'm a mess.'

She said, 'Don't be stupid, Paul, I know that already.'

A woman's standing outside the tube station with a sign that says 'Scotland Yard killed my mother.'

I want Pearl to be happy. We need happy people cause the world is so dark. Lorraine said, 'Happiness is irrelevant if you ask me.' On the news it says 'Nuclear flasks fail safety test.'

Last night the doorbell went late. I thought it might be her. I always think that. Stop thinking it, stop imagining it in such detail or it'll never be able to happen like that. It'd be too much of a coincidence. I opened the door and there was a bloke in a tracksuit with a beard. 'I was told by a geezer called John I could get a puff off you.' Pretty safe bet, John, but I don't know any Johns.

Another woman in another pub tried to give me some advice about my wife. 'If you stop wanting her she will immediately love you with a passion,' she said. 'That's how it works.'

'People repeat the same patterns endlessly,' she said. 'Endlessly. They know they're wrong but they can't help it.'

'Smirnoff Mule,' the bill board says, '– it shouldn't work but it does.' Unlike everything else in London that should work but it doesn't.

Ha.

She only loved me because I was nice to her.

Pearl and I were on the tube. There was a father with his child. The child said: 'Dad, I bet you my life savings five times over that when we get to the next stop the door will open on that side.' The father was irritated. He said: 'No, because it does. I think it does too.'

I like to think I'm a good father, but what do I know? I don't think I've got a clue. I only know that because of Pearl I try not to sink into things. If you feel that the world has no place for you, and, let's face it, most people feel that way, the temptation is to try not to think about it and live through the good things: eat, drink, buy things, have sex, take drugs, look forward to the next time you're going to eat, drink, buy things, have sex, take drugs. There's an advert above the escalators in Liverpool Street that says, 'We live in a shallow, meaningless, consumer society. Enjoy it.'

There's a billboard that says 'Don't let your lump sum become a limp sum.'

I've done stupid things. I've done loads of stupid things. Now I can't any more. My wife wanted to keep on doing what she liked. She wanted to be free. People who are wild and free cause chaos and pain and knock things over. 'They make me feel tired,' said Debbie.

I can't remember what it's like just to do what you want. I wouldn't know what it was anyway. Only that I want her to come back and that's the stupidest thing of all. If I knew where she was I wouldn't hesitate for a minute, I'd just go and throw myself at her. Put all your eggs in one basket, says Lorraine. While you're a bit sad might as well get really sad.

She once said to me: 'You know me too well. You know me so well I hate you.'

8

I don't know why but I'm not angry with my wife. But I think surely everybody needs to be shown that they're more important than at least something.

She said: 'You've got a heart as big as the moon.' Lorraine said, 'Happy people are intimidating and cruel.'

I saw a girl in a tube station. The news said: 'War in Europe.' There was a stand selling yo-yos. The girl said: 'Yes, I want a yo-yo with a light on it.' Then she burst into tears. 'Love is nothing but power games,' she said. 'Love is disgusting. I'll still take the yo-yo.'

Thank God there are so many things in the world. Otherwise there would only be me, sick with missing her.

NAOMI ALDERMAN

Gravity

ONCE, WHEN Alberto Cohen was six or seven years old, his mother took him, and Carla his sister, to the American Museum of Natural History on 81st Street. There they saw a display demonstrating what would happen to a person who fell into a black hole. Such a person would be lost for ever, crushed thinner and thinner, spun out like a strand of melted sugar towards the infinitely small centre. Those observing the phenomenon would have a different experience. For them, time would appear to cease. The unfortunate victim would seem to remain perpetually at the moment of falling, for ever alive although long dead.

'You see,' said Alberto's mother, 'this is how life is. We think we have decisions to make every day, but the real choices have been made for us, a long time ago. We are just travelling to their conclusion. It is like my life with your father. My only decision was whether to marry him or not; everything after that happened as it had to.'

It was also when Alberto was six or seven that he decided to be a writer. He admired the huge, leather-bound volumes in his father's study, and thought how fine it would be to create one of his own. He began at once, in the back of his lined school work-book and, after three hours, had created the story of a young Jewish boy living in New York who discovers he has the power to fly. The boy soars high above the city, spotting crimes being committed, and dropping stones on the heads of the wrongdoers.

When the story was complete, he showed it to Carla, who was then ten. She put down her physics textbook to read it, and when she was finished announced, rather disdainfully, that flight without wings was impossible, due to the earth's gravitational pull.

Alberto nodded, returned to his story, and rewrote it, to become the tale of a young Jewish boy living in New York, who plots to murder his sister.

Alberto's and Carla's father had been a world-famous naturalist and explorer. He had personally discovered and catalogued over six hundred types of butterfly, moth, beetle and worm in the Peruvian basin. On his final trip, he had contracted a previously unknown fungal infection. His companions had been powerless to help him and one night, in pain and delirium, he had wandered from the camp. Although Professor Cohen's body was never found, a memorial service was held in the great entomological hall of the Museum of Natural History a year after he disappeared. The service was attended by the Vice-President, and the Peruvian ambassador.

Alberto had no conscious recollection of his father. Instead, his image of him was made up of various signs and wonders.

A large portrait of the professor, half his face hidden behind a foamy tangle of beard, hung above the mantelpiece in his study, surrounded by the display cases of his prize specimens. Alberto's mother had kept the professor's last, half-smoked box of cigars in the drawer in which he had left them. When Alberto was a child, he loved to open the drawer, and inhale the aroma of the box, spicy, fresh, warm. In his mind, his father became a man of beard, with a body of insects, and the scent of unsmoked tobacco leaf.

Alberto was pleased, but unsurprised, to discover that he had a talent for writing. His schoolteachers remarked on his use of words to his mother, who reminded them that Alberto's father had been noted not only for his discoveries, but also for his impeccable writing style.

'Alberto and Carla have taken on their father's mantle,' she said, gravely.

Alberto's teachers often found him unsettling. 'He must be an imaginative child,' they said, and gave him fantastic stories to read, tales of monsters, fabulous jewels, untold riches and strange magicks. Alberto discarded them all, calling the stories made-up and unreal. Carla gave him books on plate tectonics and gravitational flux, but he found them to be even more alien.

'What does it feel like to be a planet, with molten lava churning inside?' he asked. Carla told him that the question meant nothing, and took the books away from him.

When Alberto was eleven, his story of the pain of a fatherless boy was selected as a Work of Exceptional Promise by the Writers' Guild of America. When he was fourteen, his story on the theme of adolescent alienation was published in *The New Yorker*. Alberto was not a popular young man. He found that his early success separated him from his peer group. At sixteen, he was troubled to discover that much of the abusive graffiti in the school bathrooms related to him. He composed a short series of poems on the theme, copied them, in wax crayon, onto the bathroom wall, photographed them and won a small grant from the American Humanities and Arts Foundation.

When Carla was beginning her PhD, and Alberto was

eighteen, he had a breakdown. He lay in a hospital bed for two weeks, crying. His mother cradled his head on her lap and stroked his hair, trying to comfort him. Hope came at last when she brought him a stack of *National Geographic* magazines. Amid their pages, Alberto began to understand that there were new voyages he could take, and worlds he had not yet seen.

'If we have only one life,' he wrote on a sheet of yellow legal paper, 'we must use it to pursue only that which is vital. Every moment spent on anything else is lost for ever.'

He considered the experiences that a university education could offer him and rejected them. He had read certain novels of university life and found that they centred around experiences of friendship, of sexuality, and of confusion. He decided instead to join the army.

Alberto fought in the Jungle War; three bloody and desperate years, during which he found himself daily amazed to be alive. True poetry awakened in him, and his reputation as an adult writer was sealed by his spare war verse. He was unpopular among the other soldiers, but accepted that as his lot. His poems, it was said, revealed the solitude of war, its grim calms.

Carla travelled to England, to research at Cambridge University. She was becoming increasingly interested in the earth's magnetic field, she told him in one of her letters.

'Alberto, do you realise that the earth on which you stand, and indeed on which I stand, produces magnetism? And that the magnetic poles reverse from time to time, without warning? It could happen between the time I send you this letter and the time you receive it. It could happen as you're reading it. Alberto, aren't you awed by that thought?'

Alberto read the letter and tried to understand Carla's passion. It was no good. He could no more imagine the earth's magnetic field than he could envisage a bowlful of electric soup. These things were unreal and untrue. He tried to imagine being Carla, fascinated by them, but could not. They had occasional crackly telephone conversations, the static hiss emphasising the distance between them. Sometimes she would say:

'I'm pursuing father's work, don't you see? He loved the natural world.'

Sometimes Alberto would reply:

'He loved that which he could see and touch. You're pursuing fiction.'

But mostly he would remain silent.

On receiving his discharge from the army, Alberto found himself again tempted by the university life. Several excellent institutions had offered him fellowships to teach writing, or to lecture on the writings of others. Alberto did not feel able to criticise the work of others – it would, he felt, be as absurd as criticising their eye colour. But he accepted a stipend to become writer-in-residence at a college in New England. He was only called upon to produce a small amount of prose and poetry once a year, and thought that the position might be a stabilising influence as he embarked upon his next great project.

Alberto had decided to fall in love.

He agreed to teach a seminar, just one, on Writing for Women – declaring an unending passion for the cause of women's literature. In this way, he hoped to meet women with whom he might have something in common. For Alberto had always found conversation difficult, preferring the precision and regularity of the written word.

He hoped that one of the eager young women on his course would tempt him but he found his method unequal to the task. The moment one of his pupils began to interest him, he would seize upon the emotion, take it up, analyse and dissect it. This had been his usual way, during his time in the army, and at school. It had served him well. He was surprised, therefore, to find that the more he explored his emotion of love, the less he felt it. He did not know that to love is to think only of the beloved.

But Love, from whose claws none of us escapes un-scathed, did not forget Alberto. One day, in the spring semester, as he was attempting to love Anna Mikhailovna, a brilliant Russian exchange student, his mind became disturbed. He was unable to concentrate on Anna's symmetrical features and abundant curls, because he was constantly interrupted by the face of the woman who had sold him a quarter-pound of smoked salmon that morning in the fishmongers.

He thought nothing of it, but the next day found himself unaccountably craving mussels, and was forced to make an additional journey to that same store. He could not help noticing that the young woman behind the counter had a nose that was rather oddly formed, with a bump on its left side. And her figure was insufficiently precise – her rump was rather too large and her bosom too small. Altogether unsatisfactory.

It was only after he had spent two weeks eating little but fish, and had composed an ode to the bump on Felicia's nose (for that was the name of the fishmonger's daughter), that he finally realised he had fallen in love.

As Felicia was quite as fascinated by Alberto as he was by her, Alberto was spared the cruelties of unrequited love.

Though he had hoped that he might fall in love unhappily once or twice, he found that he did not mind. Indeed, for the first time that he could recall, he felt that his art was subject to a higher calling – that of impressing his beloved.

Felicia, he felt, was rather too good for him. She was a girl of sweet and quiet temperament – uncomprehending of the darkness that causes a man to seek that which is unwholesome. Under the light of her gaze, Alberto felt himself blossom into the man she expected him to be – utterly good, utterly loving. When he met her at the fishmongers after her day was over, he would bring her pages of sonnets, quatrains, sestinas and odes. He felt, in those brief months, that he finally understood the reason for art – it was all to be gathered and laid at her feet.

He asked himself, occasionally, during that time, whether he would rather give up his art or Felicia. He was shocked to find himself unable to answer.

After a courtship lasting ten weeks, Alberto and Felicia climbed the hill overlooking the town. As they stood beneath an ash tree, regaining their breath, he fell to his knees and asked her to marry him. The sensation of relief he felt when she agreed was like a sickness lifting, or a fever passing from the brow.

They planned an autumn wedding, which became a family reunion for Alberto. His mother, older and more frail, made the journey from the City and Carla flew in from Arizona, where she had been studying ancient geological layers.

'I thought you were interested in the earth's magnetic field?' Alberto asked when they met.

'I am interested in everything that is,' answered Carla. 'How are you finding love?'

Alberto did not know how to respond – it occurred to him that his sister was becoming an old maid, that perhaps she had never experienced love. He wanted to grip her shoulder and tell her: 'Throw down your trowel! Go and find love – you will never know a power like it!'

Instead, he responded: 'I am finding it to be as inevitable and irresistible as gravity.'

Carla nodded, and seemed to understand.

Alberto's poems to Felicia were gathered into a limited edition, bound in dark red suede. Eventually, a mass-market edition was also produced, and, following publication, Alberto received, by mail, a number of unusual offers from women across the country.

Within a year, Felicia gave birth to a child: a dark-haired boy, much like Alberto himself. Alberto held the boy in his arms, and wondered, now, whether it was necessary to write at all. But, after he had given the child to its mother to nurse, and watched it snuffling, blind, for the nipple, he found words springing unbidden to his mind. By the time the second child was born, a pale-skinned girl, with blonde-white hair, he had completed two verse cycles.

After six years of marriage, Alberto found himself becoming contented. His children were growing, and seemed affectionate toward him. His life was filled with simple pleasures; the yearly blooming of the lilacs in his garden, the fresh scent of the linen after washday, the taste of butter and bread. He wrote a quiet novel of domestic happiness, exploring the tender relationship between husband and wife.

And, as the days drew on, he knew that this was the only novel he would ever be able to write about the experience of contentment. Without deciding whether Felicia would ever find out, he took a mistress, who lived in a book-lined apartment in Greenwich Village.

His mistress, whose name was Katya, smoked pink cigarettes with gold tips, and had a fierce temper. When she was in a rage, she would throw whatever was at hand, including, on one occasion, a pot of geraniums, a steak knife, the complete works of Goethe and a whole salmon, uncooked.

Alberto was powerfully excited by this tempestuous exuberance and, he noted with interest, also a little afraid. He attempted to provoke her to wilder and wilder heights of anger by acting in ways she would perceive as disdainful or uninterested. Once, in a particular fury, she hit him over the head with a cast-iron frying pan, shouting out:

'You will not even try to understand women, Alberto, because you cannot be one!'

When he regained consciousness, Katya was more emollient. Smoking a cigarette while he lay back on her green velvet-covered divan, she told him that he would not allow himself to be penetrated by life. When he asked her to elaborate, she continued:

'You think you are the one who penetrates, who pushes aside the veil with your persistent seeking for experience, but you must allow yourself to be penetrated. You will only truly experience when you can become passive, as I am.'

Alberto considered pointing out that Katya was the least passive person he had ever met, but his instinct toward self-preservation prevented him.

In private moments, though, he considered her point, and found that it had an unexpected resonance with him. He began to frequent certain bars and clubs. Eventually, one night, he accompanied a slim, dark young man to a small apartment, and allowed himself to be penetrated. He found the experience to be at once more painful and more satisfying than he had anticipated. His novella on this sensitive topic was greeted with a degree of reservation, but general approval, among the serious papers.

Alberto decided that it was time for his affair with Katya to end. He planned the matter quite deliberately. He gave her the news in her apartment. She screamed, and assaulted him with a brass coffee pot. When she was finished, he stood up, adjusted his jacket, and said, quite calmly:

'I am sorry to have caused you any distress. My greatest concern is that my wife never learns of our relationship.'

He turned, and walked briskly from the room, fearful that Katya might wrestle him to the floor once more.

Six days later, Felicia waited for Alberto in his study, early in the morning. She held a single sheet of paper in her hand. Seeing her white face, her trembling fingers, he almost wished he had never broken with Katya, or that he had never encountered her or, perhaps, that he had never asked Felicia to marry him, beneath an ash tree, out of breath.

Felicia did not explode with rage, or collapse in tears. Alberto found himself strangely impressed by her, as though, all this time, he had not really known her at all, but had only been observing the shadow she cast upon a wall, or detecting the lingering scent of her perfume after she left the room. She said:

'This is not what you have promised me.'

He felt that this sentence was perfect, that nothing could be added to it, or subtracted from it. They agreed that he should leave. He rented a large, airy, white-walled apartment across the park from their townhouse. It was an attic, with wide views across the city. He wrote Felicia's words on an otherwise blank sheet of paper and looked at them often, reading them over and over.

At this time, too, Alberto's mother died. She had passed away, it seemed, quite suddenly, sitting in the leather armchair in his father's study, holding on her knees one of the delicate display cases of Peruvian insect life. She was found by the maid, the case smashed on the carpet, neatly-labelled beetles and centipedes scattered about her feet. Alberto and Carla were saddened to find, when they arrived, that several irreplaceable specimens had been destroyed by the people who had walked back and forth in the room.

Carla had recently won a Nobel prize for her work on magnetism, and was expected in Washington to give a series of lectures. She and Alberto spent four days in the house, ensuring that everything was in order. They arranged for it to be locked up, and asked the maid to come only twice a week from now on. They agreed to return in the summer, to make some more final arrangement. If Carla noticed that Alberto did not mention Felicia's name over those four days, she did not comment upon it.

When Alberto returned from his childhood home to the white apartment, he found that the place seemed both too large and too small. He experienced an unaccountable difficulty in rising in the mornings, in ordering his days, and in concentrating his mind, matters which had never previously troubled him. While welcoming the newness of these sensations, he realised that they might signal a development which he had not anticipated. He wondered if he was about to experience another breakdown. He wrote, in desperation, forcing out more and more words, squeezing them onto the paper in lines that, for the first time in his life, seemed meaningless and trite.

He took to climbing out of his attic window, onto the grey-tiled roof, watching the people walking below, and the pigeon-society above. As though drawn there, he began to stand closer and closer to the edge of the roof. Eventually, he climbed over the rail and leaned forward, preventing himself from falling by gripping the metal barrier, his arms stretched out behind him. After observing the sensation for some time, he returned to his room, and wrote a piece which was not quite poetry, not quite prose, not quite a letter. He understood that he was unable to judge its merit, but was, nonetheless, hopeful.

The next morning, Alberto returned to the roof, and climbed over the rail. He hung, as he had done before, suspended over the city, watching. He remained there for a long while until, suddenly, it occurred to him that he might be seen there, that a crowd might gather. Disgusted by the notion, he uncurled his fingers, and gave himself to gravity.

Alberto awoke to the sight of a ceiling fan, lazily chasing round and round, white and grey on white and grey.

For a long time, all that he knew was that endless, monochrome pursuit.

At times, he saw Felicia, standing above him, red points of high colour on her cheeks. At times, she was weeping.

Eventually, the face of a doctor appeared. She spoke slowly, explaining the tiny nerves within the spine, the minute impulses with which they communicate. She told him of their delicacy, their fragility, the slowness with which they regrow, if severed. She asked him to nod if he understood. He found that he could do so.

The doctor said that he had been lucky to have survived,

that the odds were unfathomable. Nonetheless, Alberto began to wonder whether he had not, somehow, contrived it.

Alberto dreamed with extraordinary vividness. In his dreams, he ran along muddy tracks, smelling the mouldy leaves, feeling them slide beneath his feet. He ate the lightest *pain au chocolat*, the flakes crumbling on to his chin, the butter melting on his tongue. He grasped the handle of a too-hot pan, and scattered the steaming contents on a red-tiled floor.

After too much time had passed, Alberto managed to communicate to his nurses that he wished to write. A system was devised; different combinations of head gestures signified different letters. Sometimes, Felicia was his amanuensis, hiding her face behind a veil as she transcribed each painful letter.

In his last book, Alberto transcended the world with which we are familiar. His evocation of the peach took three pages; moist sunshine seemed to ooze from the paper. Reading his memory of a day of rain gave the sensation of a cold drop trickling unpleasantly down the spine.

After the book was published, Alberto received many visitors. Some reviewers came to weep at his bedside. Alberto tried to comfort them. He won many prizes; there were awkward presentation ceremonies in his room.

At last, one day in spring, he received the visit for which he had waited.

Carla took his hand in hers. He could feel the calluses in the palm of her hand, and remembered her years of digging, in Arizona. She looked older than he had expected, grey streaking her hair, her eyes lined.

'Did you know,' she asked, 'that all this may have happened before?' She did not wait for a response, but continued, softly. 'I have learned,' she said, 'that the universe itself is subject to gravity. From the first event, all matter expands, for billions of years. Life evolves, we are born, we live, we die. But the gravitational forces take over from that expansive momentum, and, like an elastic band which has stretched as far as it can go, the universe springs back in on itself, back to the first event. And the first event expands again. The same thing, over and over.

'These things which we are doing now, we have done before. We will have to go on doing them for ever. And while, the first time we did them, we may have understood our reasons, we understand no longer. Our actions, you see, are fixed. It is the reasons that we invent, Alberto.'

She looked at him, and smiled, a little.

He was sure that her words did not contain all that could be said on the matter, but knew that he could no longer attempt a response.

She said: 'Is it time?'

He nodded three times, in rapid succession. Yes.

Carla flicked one or two switches, and removed two or three tubes. She approached the bed, pulled back the sheet a little, placed her hand, very softly, over his mouth and pinched his nose shut. She waited.

MORAG MCDOWELL

Flowers in the Dark

M AUREEN HOLDS the phone to her ear, patiently counts twenty rings until it is picked up.

No one speaks but she hears the tapping of a keyboard.

'Jon?'

'Hi mum. You want to talk to Dad? He's not here.'

'It's okay, I wanted to talk to you actually, about Sunday.'

'Um, I thought it was a week on Sunday.'

'Are you studying?'

'Just looking at a website.'

'Which one?'

'Nothing you'd like. It's for my art portfolio.'

She ignores the boredom in his voice. 'Try me'

'Flowers in the Dark.'

'So are you coming on Sunday?'

'A week on Sunday.'

She says lightly, 'Okay, a week on Sunday. Two o'clock at Nico's.'

She pulls out the tutorial papers she needs to mark, switches on her computer, mulling over the scraps of conversation he's thrown her. Instead of going into her college system, she types in the name of the website he was looking at, feeling vaguely guilty, as though she's reading his secret diary. The screen fills with photos and video clips of places and people, crushed, bomb-blasted, bullet-ridden. There's a picture of an empty street where the camera is focused on a dried bloodstain on sun-bleached concrete. *Manila, 1987*. There's a young middle-eastern girl in a torn faded dress smiling cheerfully at the camera, holding up a plastic eye-patch to reveal a ragged hole where her eye should be. *Gaza City, 2001*. There's more. *Sungat, 1984*. *Hanoi, 1962*. She thinks of her son looking at these pictures, decides it's better than child pornography or bomb-making instructions and goes to close it down, but then she sees a monochrome still of a weed and razor-wire infested no man's land. She clicks on it and watches a stop motion film of a young man running, being shot, falling. *Berlin, 1969*. There is a link below to 'Berlin Wall Memories'. She clicks on it, telling herself she'll start work in five minutes.

Driving through Checkpoint Charlie was like driving off the set of a Technicolor movie and into a film noir nightmare . . .

It's an account by an ex-American Infantry man of his service posting in West Berlin in the early eighties. She scans it, only slowing down at the last four pages, which describe his experience of being 'arrested and interrogated' by the East German police following a day visit to East Berlin. She snorts with laughter at the last paragraph:

. . . they opened the gates wide for us and we walked back to freedom in the West. It's nearly a fifty yard walk through no man's land and our spines were tingling, waiting for that bullet in the back, just like in the movies.

The author's name is at the bottom: George Kochman, 6th Infantry TCA, West Berlin, 1979–82, but she's guessed that already.

Sender: MaureenMcLeod@hotmail.com
To: GeorgeK@aol.com
George Kochman, you are full of Kentucky horse-shit! I was with you – the guards were very polite, and the only bullet in the back you were likely to get that day was from me.
By the way, how are you?
Maureen

Sender: GeorgeK@aol.com
To: MaureenMcLeod@hotmail.com
Hi Maureen,
Well, I was amazed to hear from you after all this time. Your e-mail was a bit enigmatic so I'll start the ball rolling and tell you a little about what I've been doing for the last eighteen years . . .

There's two pages about his marriage, kids, divorce and a career in what he calls international security. She writes back telling him about her son, her job as a part-time lecturer at a college in Glasgow and her as yet unfinished sociology thesis which she's been writing for seven years. He replies, asking if she's ever in London and suggests they meet there while he's 'in between flights'. She tells him she's got a conference there one Friday in November and they make a date for the Sunday morning at ten o'clock in a coffee bar in Terminal 3. She stays with her friend Jo who lives in Battersea, not mentioning George until midnight on Saturday when the second empty wine bottle has clattered

26

into the bin. Jo is amused. 'So what do you actually know about this man?'

'What he told me in the e-mails. He's divorced, got two teenage kids who live with his ex-wife, he works in international security.'

'He probably cleans the x-ray machine at Louisville airport.'

'Maybe . . .'

'At least you're meeting him in a public place.'

'I knew him well.'

'Twenty years ago. And how do you know he's the real thing? Could be one of those internet stalkers, pretending to be someone else to lure you out to meet him. Are you nervous?'

'Course not. Why should I be?'

Jo nods sagely. 'I'd be nervous too. Can you remember your last meeting?'

'No. Okay yes, and I don't want to discuss it.'

'Was it that good?'

Maureen glares at Jo wordlessly. Jo shrugs. 'That's what friends are for.'

On the tube to Heathrow the next morning, she starts to recall how little they'd had in common, while the carriage grinds and shudders and rattles her hangover around inside her skull. She closes her eyes and remembers the overnight train, which carried her from Ostend to Hanover, then through the DDR. She had fifty pounds donated by her parents and a letter from a company in West Berlin offering her temporary employment at the Topler sauce and pickle factory. While most of her school friends had got engaged, or gone to work in shops or factories, she'd bought *Summer Work in Europe 1979*. All she knew about the place was gleaned from her David Bowie and Iggy Pop albums and Liza Minnelli singing 'Life is a Cabaret'.

It was the first time she'd been abroad. She hadn't been able to sleep on the train. She sat looking out at the limitless darkness while everyone around her snored, feeling the way she did when she was eight, going on the coach to Blackpool or Torquay. When they stopped at a small station before the border and a uniformed guard who looked the double of Marshall Tito switched on the overhead lights, she was the first to hand him her passport. Her smile bounced back off his face like a ball off the windows of an empty house. She wanted to ask him, 'Are we nearly there?' but told herself not to be childish, to lie back in her seat and let the train carry her to Berlin. They arrived before dawn in ZooBahn-hof where, as instructed on her letter, she got the city train to Wollankstrasse. The factory was in a residential area, about fifty yards from the wall. The woman at the reception office told her she was lucky as her shift didn't start until 5 a.m. the next morning and showed her to the temporary workers' accommodation, a grey concrete block which wouldn't have looked out of place in the council estate where she'd spent her childhood.

Most of the other workers were Irish students, who'd arrived a few weeks earlier. One of them, a dark-haired girl with freckles and knowing green eyes who introduced herself as Dervla, showed her around and told her she was working to pay her way through her second year of law studies at Galway University. Maureen asked her, 'What's Berlin like?'

'Ah it's okay, a bit sleazy, but we've been down the Irish Pub a couple of times. What made you come here then?'

She took a deep thoughtful breath and said, 'Oh, you know, the books, the films, the songs . . .,' she stopped, realising that Dervla was looking at her with pity. 'What about you?'

Dervla smiled. 'The crack, what else?'

For the first four weeks, she spent ten hours a day working, ten hours sleeping and four hours contemplating her fingers which had swollen to twice their normal size from packing tubes and jars filled with freshly boiled sauces and pickles. Then, one Friday afternoon, the payphone in the front hall rang. Someone answered it and a few moments later, the receiver was slammed down. She heard bare feet slapping on the stairs, then running down the corridor. She looked out. Dervla, dressed in bra and knickers, was battering on each door in turn. When she saw Maureen watching, she slid along the linoleum floor, slammed into her, gave her a hug, then turned and ran back down the corridor, screaming, 'Wake up girls, the Americans are coming!' Dervla and her sidekick Kate had got friendly with a couple of American servicemen stationed at the US army base at Tegel and invited them back for a drink on Saturday night. They came and brought twenty of their friends, all happy clones grinning, with jeans and pressed check shirts, army haircuts and homely accents. They came from Alabama, Mississippi, Texas, Kentucky and had either a crate of beer or a one-gallon plastic keg of Jack Daniels swinging from a well-muscled arm. George looked just the same as the rest of them, but soon stood out because he got drunk less quickly and watched quietly as the Saturday night cabaret unfolded before them. There was Dervla's repertoire of party songs which ranged from pop to paramilitary, there was Kate's exotic dancing and the boys armwrestling contests but there wasn't much conversation. Although the Saturday evening soirées became a regular fixture, they would probably never have spoken if she hadn't seen him one day reading a book. She was walking down Kurfurstendam on a rare afternoon off when she noticed him sitting at a table in a pavement café. He had a thick paperback in his hand and didn't notice as she crept up behind him, until she said, 'Caught you.'

He looked up, closing the book immediately. She read the title.

'*Moby Dick*. Did you have to smuggle that into the barracks?'

'Hell no, I told them it was a really hot porn book, oh excuse me, ma'am.'

She sat down in the chair. 'That's okay. I'm a big girl. I swear, fart, have sex, or at least I'd like to but smelling of boiled carrots and vinegar as I do, it might never happen, even though I am living in one of the most decadent cities in Western Europe. You know George, sometimes I feel like I'm not in Berlin at all. Sometimes I feel like I'm in Aberdeen after the oil was discovered.' He looked puzzled. She elaborated, 'Too many fucking Americans – no offence.'

She sat back and waited for him to say something polite and leave, knowing he'd return to the base and tell the others that one of the Irish girls was on drugs (they'd never learned to distinguish between one Celtic race and another). She saw the parties coming to an end, herself getting the blame, and realised she didn't give a damn. He closed his book and took a slow sip of coffee. 'So, you wanna go to the Bauhaus Museum?'

After that, she and George absented themselves from the Saturday night socials and went in search of the real Berlin – or at least she did, while George solicitously accompanied her. They hired a car and drove into the east for the day where she persuaded George to dump his army issue clothes because he looked like a tourist and, what was worse, an American. She bought him a cheap T-shirt and shorts and when they got arrested on the way back, she used her secondary school German to explain the situation away and secure their release. George might have been waiting for a bullet in the back, but she felt triumphant as they walked back at dusk through Checkpoint Charlie after their four-hour detention. She dragged him to night-clubs she'd read about and down derelict streets in Kreuzberg to warehouses reeking of cannabis smoke and dampness, she took him to transvestite clubs in east German housing estates, ordered him to stop opening doors for her, quizzed him about Herman Melville and, when he said, 'Who?' stopped speaking to him for a week. She stopped sending postcards of the Berlin Wall to everyone she knew, grew blasé about the gun turrets and razor wire visible a few hundred yards from the window of her room in the accommodation block. Dervla and the other girls started to assume they were an item and she couldn't help in idle moments contemplating George's US army issue washboard stomach and pectorals and thought that life with him wouldn't be unpleasant. She imagined going back with him to meet the folks in Louisville, a wedding in a white dress with the Berlin Brigade boys forming a uniformed guard of honour, a honeymoon on a cruise ship and a house with a verandah in an army compound in New Mexico. She'd fix breakfast for him and the kids then wave goodbye as he drove off in his pick-up truck to a set of iron gates in the desert where he'd spend his day checking computer printouts from missile defence systems. But she knew her future didn't lie in US army wifedom. It offended her burgeoning feminist principles and there was also the small fact that George had barely touched her. She felt relieved and insulted at the same time. Then, one night towards the end of September, they were travelling back to Wollankstrasse on the city train, the S-bahn. She preferred the rattling darkness of the old wooden carriages to the functional sterility of the underground and had wanted to travel alone, but George had insisted on accompanying her, saying he'd get a taxi back from the station to his base. They travelled in silence until, just past Wittenau, the train slowed down to a stop and the lights went out. George looked around jumpily. She decided to stop sulking and said, 'Relax. It's just a power cut . . .'

They sat on opposite sides of the carriage. George asked warily, 'Think we're the only people on this train?'

She shrugged and crossed to his side and sat down beside him. From the window on the West Berlin side there was darkness. The only light in the carriage came from the searchlights and watchtowers fifty yards away in the East. She felt him moving closer to her and said, still gazing out the window, 'What are you doing here George?'

'Defending freedom and the American Way.'

She looked at him, trying to make out the expression on his face, but he was a pattern of grey light and shadow, blending into the darkness. They both were. It could have been a black and white photograph from forty, fifty years ago, a young couple, sitting close together on an old city train, thinking they were alone, watched only by a distant lens. She put her hands up, touched his face and let her fingers run over the coarse, stubbled, line of his jaw-bone. 'You are an innocent, aren't you?'

He got up and pushed the bolt on the connecting doors to the next carriage, then came back to her smiling, his teeth gleaming uncannily white in the darkness. He took off his jacket and laid it on the narrow strip of floor in the centre of the carriage then sat on it, sinking into deep shadow. His hand stretched up. She took it and let herself fall slowly down on top of him, smelling dust and old wood and his warm faintly coffee-scented breath on her face. Her hands ran down his arms from wrist to shoulder, feeling the hairs coarse like tiny wires, brushed the soft flesh of his earlobes, tugged at the tiny buttons on his shirt and she forgot she was with George. It felt like they were strangers, disassembled and fumbling, blind men learning Braille. Afterwards, when the lights went back on and the S-bahn trundled into her station, they walked silently back to the accommodation block, where George kissed her chastely goodnight then walked back to the station to catch a taxi to the base. It was the last time she ever saw him. The next morning, she was wakened by the payphone ringing, then the sound of Dervla wailing in the distance. She wandered sleepily downstairs and saw Kate with her arms round Dervla's shoulders, saying, 'Don't worry Baby, they'll send another lot.'

He called her on the payphone later that day and told her he was being posted to Honduras. She gave him the address of her flat in Glasgow. He'd said he'd write to her in Berlin and perhaps he did, but two weeks later she got a letter forwarded to her offering her a place at a University in the north of England. She had her farewell party in the Irish pub in the Europa Centre – the girls insisted.

A tinny voice is telling Maureen over and over that she is at Heathrow Terminal 3. She jumps out just before the tube doors close and finds the coffee shop on Level 2 where they have arranged to meet. He should be there by now because it's past half ten but he isn't so she orders a coffee and drinks it, gagging at the taste. She'll give him half an hour, she thinks, and wishes the Internet had never been invented. She's picking up a discarded copy of *Hello!* in desperation, when a voice above her says, 'Caught you.'

33

She looks up, puzzled, and he's standing there, fit and lean for the forty-three which he must be, though his face looks tired and tight as though he'd just had a facelift or never eaten quite enough. She reasons to herself it's probably just jet-lag. He smiles.

'Reading a magazine.'

She remembers, says, 'I probably read more of it than you did of *Moby Dick*.'

He laughs and puts a leather flight bag on the floor. She feels like they should hug or kiss but she doesn't want to stand up and lunge across the table and he's sat down now anyway, so they exchange polite enquiries covering what they already know from the e-mails. He tells her she looks well. She tells him the same. He says, 'I'm sorry if I was late. I've got about an hour before my next flight.'

'Where are you going?'

'Louisville.'

She asks with a trace of mockery, 'International security matters?'

'We've been busy since 9/11.'

'Oh, right.' It's as though he's told her his mother died that morning. They gaze at the floor until finally she says, 'Still busy defending freedom, then?'

He smiles faintly and shrugs. 'It's a dangerous world these days. You should write a paper on it.'

His face is dead-pan. She asks, 'Have you been back to Berlin?'

'Oh sure, I go there quite a lot – Hamburg, Berlin, Frankfurt. There are a lot of sleepers there.'

'Sleepers?'

He nods. 'Algerians, Palestinians, Iraqi, Mujahedin . . . Some of them have got German citizenship. They've been living there for years, acting like good citizens, just waiting for the signal . . . I'm sorry, I'm a bit tired.'

He's fiddling with the coffee cup, head swivelling as he looks around the terminal. She sneaks a glance at his profile, the clear blue eyes, the army haircut and for a few seconds she thinks guiltily of Robert Patrick in *Terminator 2* only with black hair. She blinks the thought away and wonders if it's all real, or if he spends his life sitting behind a desk in Louisville filling in requisition forms for the State Army Facilities Division. The white noise of the airport terminal grows louder, breaks down into its separate parts – two businessmen at the next table discussing company cars, a baby somewhere screaming, a woman's voice on the airport address system appealing for Slocomo McBride to meet his sister-in-law at the enquiry desk.

He opens his mouth to say something and his flight is announced. She stands up, says, 'I'll walk you to the gate,' feeling relieved and disappointed at the same time. He picks up the small leather flight bag then drops it again. 'You know, that night on the S-Bahn. I didn't know we were going to Honduras.'

'I know.'

He picks up his bag and follows her to the walkway. 'I looked for you . . .'

They stand motionless and glide. He looks up ahead to Gate 15.

'When I got back from Honduras. I wanted to see you again so I flew to London and caught a flight up to Glasgow – just for a couple of days – thought I'd check out the address you'd given me in . . .'

'Great Western Road.'

He nods. 'That's it . . . the people there had only been

35

living in the flat for a few months . . . they were a bit puzzled, had never heard of you. I know I could have written and found out if you were there first, but . . .' He shrugs. 'Anyway, I put a few notices in the local papers, *The Herald*, *The Evening Times*, with a box number just in case.'

'Just in case.'

She doesn't mean it to sound sarcastic, but she can feel him watching her and she's thinking of Robert Patrick again, imagining the heat sensor readings of her face, the digital display 'scanning for true feelings' in flashing red letters. They step off the walkway. The flight has started boarding. He gives his ticket to the girl at the gate, whose bright smile is a rictus of impatience. He turns to her and shrugs. 'It was a long shot and now you think I'm crazy, right?'

She shakes her head, imagining him running at the speed of light through a bombed-out futuristic landscape, searching for evil, fighting for freedom, but then she remembers that in *Terminator*, the terrorists are the heroes. The ticket girl says, 'The flight is closing now, sir.'

He says, 'I'm sorry.'

She laughs and asks, 'Why?' but he's already walking down the gangway. She takes the lift to the viewing deck, counts twenty take-offs until she thinks he's probably in the air then walks to the gate for her flight home. She telephones Jo that night, as promised. Jo listens then says in a blurred voice, 'Do you think he's for real?'

'What do you mean?'

'Hello Miss Gullible, you don't believe all that international anti-terrorist stuff do you?'

'Maybe.'

Jo starts to laugh. It takes two minutes before she stops.

She's still sobbing and gasping with mirth when Maureen says, 'You're a cynical drunken old hag.'

'You are absolutely right, my lamb. So what are you going to do?'

Maureen feels her ears pop as the plane starts to descend. There's a small electronic buzz and the pilot says, 'Good evening Ladies and Gentlemen, we will shortly be landing in Schonefeld where the weather is clear and local temperature approximately 16 degrees centigrade. If you look out of your windows on the right you can see the Brandenburg Gate which just a few years ago was reopened as a main route for traffic in Berlin.'

The city is spread out below her in the darkness, streamers of main roads flowing out from the one bright central point. She tries to imagine what it had looked like before from up here, with no man's land and the Eastern sector dimmer than the rest like a daisy of light with petals ripped away. She closes her eyes and sees her son's face lit by a computer screen, gazing at images of villages exploding into flames, the stain of blood on a far-away pavement, then it's Jo lying glass in hand on her sofa in a red silk dressing-gown with the room lights out. She blinks, reaches into her pocket and takes out the print of an e-mail she sent two days earlier. She reads it over and over again, wondering what she'll find in the unknown city below her.

To: GeorgeK@aol.com
From: MaureenMcLeod@hotmail.com
George,
Did we ever find the real Berlin? They say these days you can look all the way down from Kleiner Stern through

the Brandenburg Gate to Unter Den Linden. Cafe Lebensart. 2.30 p.m., Thursday 10th January 2002. Maybe I'll see you there.
Maureen

MORAG MACINNES

The Scotswoman's Pillow Book

Y OU SHOULD try lists, the new lady doctor said. Count
your blessings. In for a penny in for a pound, eh? They
all talked this kind of claptrap. This blethering. But the lists
gathered in spite of the blether. So:

Things to be sad about
1 all three bodies were on the gutting deck
2 the big success of Taste the Fare was the Smoked
   Mackerel Cakes Thai Style
3 there are hardly any gardens on Skye
4 Fraserburgh
5 nobody knits you pixie hoods any more

Things to be glad about
1 all three bodies were on the gutting deck
2 digging up the tiniest tatties
3 how the town is uglier than when I was a child
4 wind will always try to get into a house
5 the dream about hitch hiking the A9 with Kenny and the
   biscuit van

These lists were written by Thelma on bits of paper. She
regretted them mostly. You don't give out stuff. Especially
about death and love, people will only get their scratchy wet
pens on your file.

There's a lot to be said for knitting, which keeps the hands obedient and the head full of rows.

Laura is a small squat square lass with a flat face and short hair all gelled. She has some spots. Her father is a drunk and doesn't live with her mother. Laura likes her men to be over thirty. She eats a lot of cakes and calls salad rabbit food. She has to smoke in cars because she gets sick otherwise. Thelma knows all this about Laura because she listens to her talking to the nurses and the other people, the cleaners and the trolley pushers. Thelma knows about everybody because she has been in the Place for years, since she decided not to talk or bother.

Bother means bother going anywhere, like the toilet or the kitchen.

'Some stuff you wrote, you daft cow,' said Laura. 'There'll be a case conference now, you should have kept your big mouth shut.'

I never opened my mouth, thought Thelma. Which you wouldn't notice for you never have yours shut. I won't be talking about pixie hoods will I? Or gutting decks or the A9? It didn't get spoken, only written, daft cow yourself.

'Don't you give me that evil eye,' Laura said from under her spiky helmet.

Things which disgust
1 the dirt around light switches
2 how seals bite a fish and throw it back ruined
3 hair caught in your teeth
4 the smell of your fingers just out of the priest's tobacco pocket
5 and the sweetie pocket

'Old bitch,' Laura said in the night. 'Dirty Pape.' Or else Thelma dreamed it.

Laura cut herself and starved herself which was why she was in the Place, and once she got out she said she would get a Death By Chocolate catering pack and some deep frozen Snickers and go to the big high waterfall that said Viewing Point Do Not Look Down and eat them all and then sick them all up till she lost her voice with all the honking. Her mother tried to stop the eating and honking and starving and cutting but you can't run a hotel with no knives. You can't always have your eye on the fridge either. Realistically speaking.

Laura's arms look like she's written runes on them. Or bar codes.

Sometimes she talked all night at Thelma. Sometimes she shouted out Thelma's lists.

'What a giveaway, fucking notes all over everywhere, fucking crap poetry,' she yelled. 'What's so clever, anybody could do it, make lists, get better, talk of the fucking town, I could do it.'

Laura uses words like fucking and arse and cunt all the time. This, which must be how girls talk now, worried Thelma. Not that she bothered. Laura's business, how she says things. Thelma gave up on other people's business a long time ago, as soon as she saw there was nothing she could do about it. She concentrated on herself. But she did wonder whether Laura was right and the lists were a sign of something moving round about her. She watched her knitting bag for a while. It seemed quite settled.

Writing might be more trouble than it was worth, being the next thing to talking. Like when Laura bought up all the sweeties on the Sally Anne trolley and the wee lady said, 'A minute on the lips a lifetime on the hips hen' to her. Words could leap into your mouth like sweeties and there'd be a lifetime of regret to follow, she'd be all fat with words again. You will have to watch yourself, my joy, thought Thelma to her twitchy writing hand.

The trouble was that after Laura had talked herself hoarse nights and then dropped suddenly to sleep Thelma found herself observing the dawn with some interest. It was the colour of dirty water, but it had a relentlessness. She wrote:

Things which bring a sudden rush of joy
1

She stroked it out but started it again.

Things which bring a

'See him that comes in the van that's my latest squeeze, he's a great fuck,' Laura said. The wind was battering about. Thelma found herself waiting.

He was very dark-haired and red-faced and heavy-set. His boots were oily boots or Council, good quality work. Thelma looked and then was angry with herself for getting interested in the great fuck. She had nearly been clock-watching, and she didn't like that, she wanted to say, move me away or I'll shift myself.

'Give us a tit,' he said, 'let me have a feel of a fat wee tittie.'

'Who are you calling fat, fat bastard,' said Laura.

'I'm away Sunday. Give us a wee feel.'

'Were you up the Arms?'

'Aye.'

'Nothing doing?'

'No. Aye. Big Jim got the boot. Fi – nally.'

'Nicking?'

'Aye.'

'Did you walk the dogs?'

'No.'

'Ah they'll be bursting, gonny walk them?'

'Whose dogs is it?'

'My good wee doggies.'

'Aye well. You walk them.'

In the night Laura told Thelma she had hung a deer in the hotel shed until it was green and minging, and crawling. Then she had to wash it down with vinegar and it came to pieces in her hands.

'That's how it's meant to be. Stinking. Then we cooked it, for the gets.'

Gets are guests. If Laura were to write a list of enemies, Thelma thought, she would write down 1 The Environmental Health 2 English vegetarians.

But anyway. Things which bring a rush of joy.

There must be some.

Some squealing for sure when Laura gets the dressings off her arms; nobody can hear the telly. On the plus side, she is quieter at night because there is plenty to pick at. She will be going out soon, in her old waxy jacket, in her trainers, into the rain.

Surprises, wrote Thelma, on the back of Puzzle Monthly.

1 the air smells a different pine smell in here if you open the
   window

'Can you no get five on your list, creepy wife?' said Laura
at ten past three. Thelma was finding the dawn a bad time
since she had started noticing it.

'What about fucking old men, that's a surprise, or
Pernod, or Walnut Whips, or that awful nice Doctor
Mackie's awful nice son breaking the hippy shop window.
Or a bit dry weather, that's a surprise. I tell you what's
surprise, a Jehove handed me a card outside the Post Office,
it said the hand of God stretches out to you, it was orange.
That was a surprise. The last hand stretched out to me was a
right wanker.'

Thelma had been considering coming across a cow in the
dark in the old Anglia, and whether that was as surprising
as being sent a stone, just a stone in a box. She was cross at
the interruption. Pernod led to milk and licorice, which led
to furry teeth and a sick stomach and the not-so-Holy
Fathers. It also led to pictures of Laura. In her trainers in
the rain swearing, stuck without a taxi on a Saturday night
because the drivers on the island know she's a daft wee cow
and won't shift themselves at 2 a. m. to pick her up. Runes
on her arms like the bad words carved in the Ladies outside
the Copie Shop. Washing down green meat with a vinegary
clout on a hungover midge-ridden morning. Walking the
dogs in the dark because they're vicious bastards.

It was too much, having to think about other people.
And a bit unfair if pictures of real people started coming
just when you were trying to make your own personal
wee life list. The experiment was a mistake. Even her
knitting bag looked as if it might up sticks and elope with

the Gideon Bible into the quivering dawn. Thelma decided she would stop wondering about what was happening up the Arms and whether the dogs had been peed. I have to concentrate on myself, one way or another, she thought.

But everybody in the whole Place got the Laura treatment when they let her out, because oily man came in the van with the dogs all yowling and scrabbling. Right parked up on the front step and a can of Carlsberg in his hand, ready open for her.

'Bye bye mad fuckers! Only kidding! Bye bye folks!' she shouted. 'Cheerie-bye! Shut UP you stinkin mingin dogs.'

And then the view was less demanding. Thelma went back to ravelling and unravelling, knit one slip one. The dawn went back to being punctuation on the wall. You could call that lassie a surprise, she thought. Not joy, but surprise. She did not commit anything of the sort to paper just in case. Puzzle Monthly went off to be recycled. At ten past three most nights, when the pine smell in the window crack was strongest, though, she felt a funny feeling. It was like missing something.

Up the Arms, Laura covers her paper with her bar-code arm as she writes, just like she did at school. Nobody is looking, but just in case. She puts:

Things to do
1 defrost the big freezer (sad)
2 get right liver for the dogs (glad)
3 give the squeeze a haircut (surprise)
4 Walnut Whips for the Thelma wifie

There's no time for number 5, because the squeeze starts singing Willie Nelson awful well and everybody has to show respect – but she'll do it later, probably.

KAMILA SHAMSIE

Horatio's Story

T HE EVENING of our dress rehearsal, there was a military
coup.

'It's that bitch prima donna!' the director declared, when
the news broke. 'She's the one behind this. Just because I
didn't cast her as Gertrude. That bitch and her bastard
husband!' With that, she threw a freshly printed brochure
on to the stage and stormed out of the theatre.

Claudius bent down, buttons of his military uniform
straining to stay closed across his daily-spreading stomach,
and picked up the brochure. On the cover was a picture of
the cast in military regalia – including Gertrude and Ophelia
– saluting sharply at Claudius, while Hamlet sulked off to a
side in jeans and a 'PEACE' T-shirt.

'Bugger,' Hamlet said. He said it as though it were
iambic. His affectations were increasing daily, and Fortinbras' men had more than once threatened to drop him on
his head as they carried him off-stage in the final scene.

'I told her we should have done *The Importance of Being
Earnest*,' the producer said, rolling up his sleeve and slapping on two nicotine patches.

Two chairs in the front row started jigging up and down.
Many of us had left our mobile phones there, on silent, and
as news of the coup spread across the city they started
vibrating furiously, setting up mini-tremors. We were all

on-stage, having gathered for a pep-talk before starting the performance. Hamlet was the only one among us who hadn't been warned on pain of death to move carefully so as to avoid creasing his sharply-ironed military uniform, so he was the only one to leap off the stage to answer the phone.

'No!' said the producer, catching Hamlet by the back of his T-shirt, while he was still in mid-flight. 'We don't speak to anyone until we've decided what to do here. Turn those phones off. I'm going to find out what I can about our new leader.' He turned sharply on his heel – the entire crew had been infected by the actors' militaristic movements over the last weeks – and walked to the sound booth, where he kept both his phone and his hipflask.

'Wonder what kind of dictatorship it'll be this time,' Ophelia said, lighting up a cigarette.

Polonius shrugged. 'For the first few weeks it's safe to be as paranoid as possible.' Polonius was only eighteen (he'd been the prompter until yesterday when the actor who had been rehearsing for the part of Polonius fell into the wings while being stabbed by Hamlet and broke his leg) but he was in make-up and his artificially hollowed eyes and white hair gave him the air of one who has lived through multiple coups.

'Does she really think this has something to do with her casting decisions?' Fortinbras asked, jerking his thumb in the direction the director had gone.

There had been more than a little name-calling, six weeks earlier, when the director refused to cast one of her former classmates in the role of Gertrude, even though the woman had more theatrical experience than the rest of the amateur cast put together. No place for prima donnas in my play, was all the director said by way of explanation. The classmate's husband was a general in the army, and we had all decided that the director's decision to set a play beset with intrigue and murder in a military world was a further dig at the prima donna who never tired of talking about the integrity of her husband's chosen career.

The theatre door rolled open on its castors and the director walked back in, her jaws moving as though she were rapidly chewing gum – by now we had all come to recognize her air-mastication as a sign of agitation. 'Well, that's it, isn't it? That's just it. We're going to need some divine intervention now. Come on God, work your magic.'

'NO SUCH LUCK' a deep voice boomed over our heads.

We looked up to the sound booth. The producer was bent over, speaking into the mike. 'JUST GOT A CALL FROM THE THEATRE MANAGER. THEY CAN'T RISK OFFENDING THE ARMY NOW. THE PLAY'S OFF UNLESS WE DROP THE WHOLE MILITARY ASPECT.'

Loud exclamations of horror from the wardrobe team, the set-designers, and – in particular – Claudius, who had only just perfected his salute.

'But we'll never get another set of brochures printed in time for tomorrow's performance,' Laertes pointed out. When Laertes wasn't Laertes, he worked in human resources in a multi-national company which was advertising its services on the back cover of the brochure.

'But soft,' said Hamlet.

Fortinbras' men looked at each other and mimed tossing a body off-stage and into the audience.

'The irony of Fortinbras's "Bear Hamlet like a soldier to the stage" speech gets completely lost unless I'm the only one in civvies through the play.'

'Sweetheart, it worked for Shakespeare,' said Ophelia, blowing smoke rings in the air.

The theatre door opened again, and the twins – Rosencrantz and Guildenstern – sauntered through. 'It's not Act II yet, is it?' one of them asked.

'No, it's curtains for us,' said Polonius, and then looked around quickly to ensure we'd all got the joke.

'THERE'S BEEN A COUP.'

Ros. and Guild. waved up to the sound booth. 'We know. Our uncle's the new man-in-charge.'

By now most of us had lost our military bearings and were draped over chairs or leaning against the backdrop, but the twins' assertion had us bolt upright again.

'Really? So do you think . . . it's okay for the production to go ahead, as is?' The director's jaws were working furiously now.

Rosencrantz and Guildenstern looked confused for a moment, and then turned to each other with expressions of horror.

'Oh,' said one.

'Shit,' said the other.

'What?' we demanded.

'He's coming to watch it tomorrow.'

'Huh?' some of us said.

'Who?' the rest of us said.

'Uncle. We just spoke to him. He thinks it's important to appear as though he's in command and without worries. And we said, any man who's willing to fly down from the capital to sit through a three-hour production of *Hamlet* the day after he comes to power cannot be accused of worrying about being overthrown.'

While the rest of us were attempting to form opinions about the logic of this remark, the director tried to find a lifeline and grab it. 'And if the play has the villainous Claudius as the head of the army, and the real head of the army is able to watch that without having us all thrown into prison it's a further sign that he's secure in his position, right?'

The twins shook their heads. 'Uncle is very sensitive.'

'Oh come on,' said the Ghost/Osric/Gravedigger, waving his hand in a gesture that dismissed military coups, theatre managers, and the sensitivity of relatives. 'Uncle isn't going to accept your invitation to watch the play you're in, and then end up arresting everyone involved, is he? That's not very familial.'

But the twins shook their heads again. 'Having us arrested would allow him to show the world he's a man who rises above nepotism. Good PR is very important for dictators, these days.'

'And also, he's never liked us.'

Gertrude touched my wrist, lightly. 'Here we are again. Older, and infinitely less brave.'

She said it so softly only those closest to her would have heard, but everyone fell silent as her body leaned towards mine and I looked away.

Gertrude and I had been at university together, some fifteen years earlier, when the bloodiest of the military coups took place. Then, too, we'd been in the process of staging a play – but that play had been written by me, with Gertrude in a minor role as Peasant Woman. A prescient play, it would have been called, if we'd staged it just a few days earlier. It was a satire aimed at the civilian government, and through the play the sound of army boots marching off-stage got louder and louder until in the final moments it drowned out the voices of the actors completely.

But it never had a chance to play in front of an audience. Ten days before opening night the coup occurred, and one of the first acts of the new leader was to imprison the country's most famous poet on the charge of treason. The university chancellor came personally to our rehearsals to say the play was off. He was clearly in no mood to be argued with so I merely suggested that we perform another play I'd just finished writing – a love story.

He held his forefinger up sternly, almost poking out my eye with it. 'Nothing written by you. Nothing. Not one word. You'll get us all thrown into jail.' The Chancellor was not as stupid as he sometimes appeared. My love story centred around a pair of revolutionaries.

'So should we return all the tickets we've sold?' said Gertrude/Peasant Woman.

It was a masterful remark. The Chancellor was well aware that the tickets had already sold out. (I am by nature a modest man, but it would be fact, not bragging, to say that my reputation as a playwright contributed to the rapid sales of tickets and compelled us to add an extra night's performance to our four-day run. At twenty-two I already had a number of successful and critically acclaimed television plays to my credit, and there was talk of naming the university's drama award in my honour as soon as I graduated and stopped winning it myself.) The Chancellor's finger wavered. He'd already earmarked the profits from the play for new equipment for the chemistry labs, as part of his attempts to woo the new chemistry professor.

'Put up a sign saying tickets sold cannot be returned, and do another play,' he said. 'But nothing written by you –' and here he actually jabbed his finger into my forehead. 'Nothing written by anyone local. Nothing controversial. Do Shakespeare.'

So we did Shakespeare. *Julius Caesar*. In contemporary, local dress. Every scene informed by paranoia and corruption. We ended with Mark Antony's funeral oration – the crowd brought around to his side not by his words but by Octavius' jackbooted men, already in the city, who slip through the crowd as Antony speaks and offer gold to those who will cry themselves hoarse in support of the ex-playboy who is having his lines fed to him by Octavius' speechwriter, who stands behind Antony and whispers in his ear.

I played Antony. Gertrude/Peasant Woman was the speechwriter. Opening night, the crowd gave us a standing ovation that went on so long our backs were exhausted with the repetitive bowing and straightening. The next day the Chancellor was removed from his position, and I was arrested, along with Gertrude/Peasant/Speechwriter, who was in my bed when they came to take me away.

The next six months, in prison, I will not speak of. But suffice it to say I hadn't written anything since, and only took the part in this production of *Hamlet* because Gertrude said she wanted me to, and fifteen years later I still didn't know how to look at her and form my mouth into the word 'no' at the same time. And also, to be entirely frank, I took the part because the currents of my blood no longer anticipated the tide of political fortunes, and so I was quite unaware this time of the sound of army boots marching closer and closer to the seat of power. Whether the same was true of Gertrude, I cannot say.

And now they were all looking at me, and remembering who I had once been.

'What can we do?' the director asked me.

'Er, why are you, um, asking him?' Hamlet said. Hamlet, Polonius and Ophelia were the only ones young enough to have no memory of the reputation I had once held; the other two had doubtless heard the old stories when the cast and crew gossiped away their off-stage time, but Hamlet himself never mingled with the rest of us and so was likely to have no knowledge of my past. He would have said his solitary state existed because he preferred using that time to meditate, but the truth of it was that none of us liked him at all and saw no reason to strike up conversation with him.

As I heard his voice (the 'er' and 'um' in his sentence a pathetic attempt to control the metre of the line), it was my dislike for him rather than anything else that made me say to the director, 'Make Claudius the hero of the play.'

There was a moment of silence, and then Ophelia stubbed out her cigarette and laughed. 'Cool,' she said.

'Make Claudius the hero,' I repeated to the director, who had that look of panic that comes to people who aren't sure if they've heard something brilliant or stupid, and are all too aware that their manner of response will reveal the quality of their own intelligence. 'That way you can leave in the military stuff. Claudius as hero, and Hamlet as the villain – or perhaps just the profoundly misguided fool – who is trying to overthrow him. We can present it as a morality tale dissuading acts of treason against the military.'

Gertrude's voice behind me was confused, yet hopeful. 'And what's the twist?'

I couldn't look at her. I looked instead at Hamlet, who had turned purple at the mention of 'misguided fool' and said, 'There is no twist. That's the story. A fool thinks the military leader should be deposed, and in killing him he wreaks havoc on everyone's lives, including his own. Let that be our *Hamlet*. Twins, will Uncle like that?'

'Uncle will be delighted.'

And so it was agreed upon. I said I needed a little time and solitude to re-work the script, and so I left them (the director pulled Gertrude back when she would have followed me), walked to my parking spot and got into my car.

I didn't turn on the ignition, merely placed my hands on the steering wheel, holding a copy of the script between them, and tried to remember how to adapt a play for the need of the hour.

It was, after all, remarkably easy. This is what I did: I made the ghost left-handed.

When the ghost beckons Hamlet to follow him I gave Horatio these words: My lord, the left. He beckons with the hand/of devils and of wraiths. In life he was/right-handed.

Hamlet, silly bastard, doesn't pay any attention: Horatio, can you expect/transforming Death to leave a man unchanged?

Of course, our local audience would know that the left hand denotes that this ghost is the devil's work. Once I had that in place, the rest was easy. If the ghost is sent by the devil demanding Claudius' death than Claudius must be the hero. (His gracious decision to marry his brother's widow in accordance with the customs of our nation only furthered his heroic status.) All the play needed after that was a little chopping and changing. When Claudius runs out of 'The Mousetrap' demanding a light, Hamlet thinks that's the sign of a guilty conscience but the audience would be aware (helped along by the addition of an aside from Claudius) that the acting is terrible and the king is falling asleep amidst the darkness and the hamming up. So when Hamlet informs him that 'You shall see anon how the murderer gets the love of Gonzago's wife' he realizes the play isn't over, not by a long stretch and he just can't bear the thought of sitting through any more over-acting so he bolts from the room. The king is a man with strong feelings about Bad Art.

That taken care of, I removed all asides/soliloquies in which Claudius admits to a guilty conscience, removed the bit about Hamlet finding a letter ordering his death, and then the good king was recreated as a man concerned about his troubled step-son/nephew/heir, whose every action is misinterpreted by the devil-duped, murdering prince. I also chopped out chunks of Hamlet's soliloquies, just to irritate him.

The cast was enthusiastic when I returned indoors – less than an hour later – with my idea. It would require only minor adjustments to the script and would keep us all out of jail. Only Hamlet sulked. Gertrude said nothing, and kept her face turned from me. Perhaps she was grateful, and unwilling to admit it.

We rehearsed through the night. Claudius was a revelation to us all – as the villain of the piece he'd been unconvincing, but as hero he filled the stage with such nobility and sense of purpose that by midnight Ophelia declared that even if the civilian government returned to power before our opening performance we would have to continue with this new version of *Hamlet*. And then the actors – all except Gertrude and Hamlet – formed a circle around me and applauded, and when I wept they thought it was for joy.

We went home to sleep in the middle of the morning, and when we returned to the theatre in the evening, each of us was stunned to see 'OPENING NIGHT SOLD OUT' scribbled across the posters near the theatre entrance. Each of us, that is, except Laertes, who had seen the marketing possibilities in spreading the word that our new leader would be at the play; in the last few hours, journalists for news agencies across the globe had snapped up the (many) available tickets.

The new leader sat in the front row, of course – on either side of him were his daughters, whose ample bodies and voluminous clothing conspired to form a shield which made it impossible for any of the journalists to glimpse his expression through the play. But we could see him – when the play started we were all (except Bernardo and Marcellus) gathered together in the wings, almost falling over ourselves as we peered out into the audience to see his reaction as the curtains opened to reveal the two men in uniform, standing with rifles drawn outside military headquarters. His brows drew together.

'I can't,' I found myself whispering. Old scars along the length of my body started to ache. A premonition of rain? Not this time, I didn't think. 'I can't,' I said again, and turned to make my escape. But it was my cue, and the others were jostling to make room for me, carving a passage to the stage. Gertrude caught my eye, and opened her mouth to speak, and it was only to escape her that I turned and walked into my role.

When I looked at our leader again, just after those crucial lines about the left-handed ghost, he was yawning. I took that as a good sign.

But when Claudius appeared on the stage, he sat up again, and at first his face was grim, but when Claudius – impromptu – stepped aside from the assembled crowd for a moment, locked eyes with our new leader and let his shoulders slump with the weariness of a man on whom an entire nation depends, our leader put his hand up to his eyes, and bowed his head slightly.

When it all ended, our leader applauded with enthusiasm. Reports conflicted about whether he'd really winked at Ophelia, but there was no doubting that we were off the hook, even if we'd gravely offended those in the audience who had come to see the *Hamlet* which Shakespeare had written.

I went home, relieved and miserable.

It couldn't have been more than a couple of hours after the play ended that I turned on one of the international news channels. For the first few minutes I drifted in and out of the reports from around the world, thinking only of Gertrude, wondering why we had never spoken of that night we'd spent together, wondering why we'd never spoken of all those months in our separate prisons, wondering why she'd got engaged so quickly after her release from captivity and whether I had been a gentleman or a coward in my willingness to fall into the role of old college friend, nothing more, as soon as my own release was secured, weeks before her wedding. And wondering, particularly, after all these years why she had called me up and asked me to return to the stage beside her?

And then, the stage was in front of my eyes. On the television, with footage from the evening's performance. There was Hamlet, saying, 'The play's the thing, wherein I'll catch the conscience of the king.' And then, there was a reporter I recognized from the audience, describing our *Hamlet* as 'not only making a strong statement of political protest, but doing so in front of the President – with such subtlety that he applauded at the end with no idea of what he had just seen. But to the rest of us it was perfectly clear that the play was an indictment of censorship – in the current atmosphere of uncertainty here you can't even perform *Hamlet* without changing and chopping in ludicrous fashion to appease the government.'

It didn't occur to me to be worried, until the news anchor asked, 'Is it possible the adaptation really was just an attempt at appeasing the military?' and the reporter answered, 'No, if you consider who made the changes to the script, it's clear this was a very well-thought out piece of political satire.' And then he launched into that fifteen-year-old tale of my political courage and subversion.

I phoned Gertrude, but there was no response. So I called the director instead.

'I was about to phone you. Pack a bag,' she said, in the tone she used to tell us how to deliver a line. 'I've spoken to the twins. Uncle is furious. He saw the first news report, just minutes after the play ended. He wants to arrest us all. Each one of us, especially you. But he has a dilemma.'

'Oh, thank God,' I said.

'On a national level, he wants to discourage acts of treason – which is, incidentally, how he has taken to referring to our play. But on an international level, he doesn't want to be seen as a man who arrests an entire group of performers within twenty-four hours of taking office. Also, he's feeling like an idiot and he just wants the whole thing to go away.'

'Fine. Great. So we cancel the rest of the run.'

'And we leave the country.'

'Sorry?'

'Otherwise he'll have to arrest us to make an example of us. For the local audience, you see. The only way out, he said – he called Claudius to discuss this, not the twins – is for all of us to get on a plane before dawn and leave. The official story is that we got a last-minute request to perform *Hamlet* – the original version – at a festival in foreign parts. He's arranging for some foreign part to allow us into the country. All this is hush-hush. Tomorrow morning, he's going to be officially-unofficially in a rage about our escape.'

I didn't quite follow, and I suspect the director didn't either because she told me I had no time for questions. So I packed a bag and went to the airport.

Within a short space of time, we were all there, sequestered in the VIP lounge. All except Gertrude. No one had been able to get through to her. I tried to leave the airport to go in search of her, but a uniformed, armed man blocked the doorway and wouldn't let me pass. I kept on calling until my finger ached from punching the re-dial key.

And then, just minutes before we were to board the plane – to where, we still didn't know – her husband answered her mobile.

'It's you,' he said, and in those two words he told me something he'd never told me before – that he knew. That I had loved her, that she had spent the night with me, and more perhaps. Perhaps he knew if she had loved me, too.

'Can I . . . ?' I said.

'No. None of us can. She's dead.'

She had killed herself.

I whispered 'Dead? What?' and in the responses of everyone around me – those expressions of grief mingled with utter knowing – I realized I had been the only one who had failed to see her looking at her life and wondering why she held on to it.

He was still talking. My rival, now suddenly my brother. 'There was nothing anyone could have done. She'd been so close to doing it so many times before, for so many years. How is it those months in prison destroyed every particle of hope in her, and allowed you to carry on living so easily? Each day for her was a struggle to find a reason to go on. I've always known there'd be a day when she wouldn't find that reason.'

Fifteen years of clues that I had done nothing but misinterpret flamed to life in my mind. Those faraway looks of hers, those marks on her wrist, those comments that made no sense because I didn't want to see the sense behind them, those months when she disappeared from view and wouldn't even answer phone-calls, that hopefulness with which she said 'And what's the twist?' as though she saw a way to relieve herself of the burden of finding that day's reason.

And still he was talking. 'When I found her, she was delusional. She thought she was still in the play. Gertrude dying on-stage. But she messed up her lines, or rather, her role. She looked straight past me and said, "If thou didst ever hold me in thy heart, absent thee from felicity awhile. And in this harsh world draw thy breath in pain."'

The decision I made, right away, came to mind with the familiarity of an old thought, one entirely aware of its origins, its justifications, its (my scars ached again) repercussions.

I embraced each one of the players in farewell, and was surprised by the tenderness with which Hamlet, more than any of the others, held me. 'How easily we turn from hero to misguided fool,' he said, the iambs of the line utterly natural. 'How much harder to turn back. And how much braver.' Then he kissed me on the cheek and pulled away, my tears a sheen on his lips.

I stayed in the lounge to watch the plane depart, aware of the uniformed man watching me from the doorway as he spoke into a mobile phone, my name the only words I could make out in his whispered conversation.

The plane rose higher and higher, graceful against the rising sun.

JANE MALTBY

An Angel in the Garden

S HE KEPT finding bits, all over the place, even after they'd
cleaned up. Not from the victim, of course not, that
would be silly, although he went straight out through the
windscreen and along the road, face down, they told her.
She didn't look. Even when all the neighbours ran down
their gardens to the road, and all the police cars with their
lights were parked all over the grass, and it was even on the
radio, the cars were queued up for that long.

The boy's car had embraced the lamp-post deeply. That
was the thought that struck her. It had sucked the post into
its vitals. Glass and metal lay on the ground, and these were
the bits that, weeks after the crash, she kept crunching over
when she finally went down, to check the flowers. The body
had come to rest perhaps twenty yards away, just on the
boundary with her neighbours, who kept cats. Just inside
the boundary. It was her accident, all right.

The flowers appeared the next day, when the car was
gone. At first, it was just one bunch, carnations in stiff
cellophane, and they had been attached somehow to the
lamp-post. She went to check: they had been tied on with
string. More bunches appeared over the next week, sell-
otaped or tied or simply stuck in because there were that
many, it began to look like a florist's shop front by the end
of a few days. Carnations and roses and baby's breath and

daffodils because it was early in the year. Lilies, a few. Cryptic messages wrapped in plastic and stapled to the cellophane: 'Miss you, see you round the table up there.' 'My golden boy, always.' 'With deepest sympathy, the boys in bay six.'

The flowers, top-heavy, leaned out at crazy angles. She would look out, several times a day, out of the bay down towards the ring road where the cars sped past, or crawled past, depending on the hour, and see the flowers cartwheeling, drunkenly, round the post. It was annoying. Untidy. She hadn't asked for her lamp-post to be chosen, for a young man to die at the end of her garden.

Bodies deserve dignity, and that was why she hadn't joined the rush to look at the hole in the windscreen, and the smear of blood on the road, even though it was her lamp-post where the car had come to rest. Why that one? She looked at it from her window, at the cars racing past. She shook her head, mouth puckering, as always. The ring road.

When she and her husband had bought the house the road was a track, really, that led west and east from the big road leading north out of town, along the fields to the old farm. The farmer sold off the fields for these houses, which were expensive, but her mum left them some money, otherwise they'd have been right over the other side of town. It was always quiet, the cattle behind them and the birds out front. Although the cattle were sold, and then the farm and then, years later, the town was by-passed altogether, and the road was sent right past the houses, thousands and thousands of cars a day running past the bottom of her garden. And on the other side of town the council built a park, and a leisure centre, and a nice supermarket, so they would have been better off there all along, especially after her husband passed on, and with him the car.

She was still working when he died, and she would walk down the garden to the ring road, turn left, ignoring the traffic, walk to the main road, and catch the bus into town. There were accidents all the time, but she never stopped to look. It wasn't the body that she shied away from: twenty years in a doctor's reception fortified you against most diseases and ailments, and a lot more efficiently than antibiotics. Indeed, people did terrible things in doctors' surgeries, as if all the – this wasn't the word, but it would do – coverings of society were taken off there, in that dry, cracking heat. Old radiators. Peeling paint. People pushed their bare naked faces up against the glass demanding help, and if you weren't quick enough – if a doctor was late, or ill, or the time wasters had slipped past your vetting system and all the appointments were queuing up, like the cars at the end of the garden in rush hour – the most ugly, accidental things could happen. People were sick on the floor, or they fainted or worse. She had watched the kiss of life, several times, right there in her reception. She had seen the bodies of old men slide off their chairs, backside first, the heart not willing to wait any longer. It was their time, that's all, their pattern worked out. Once or twice there was blood: in would come a huge dog, or that girl with the nose-ring and the Stanley knife, and the worst would happen. The dog's torn ear, the nose-ring, these were clues as to what might come to pass, but the doctors didn't notice those sorts of things. They were too busy being even-handed and non-discriminatory, as she read in the leaflet they gave her once. They never judged. But they never had to scrub the floor afterwards, either.

At lunchtime, she would do a crossword: whatever had

been dropped off that morning. One day it would be a celebrity glossy, and the next a caravan owners' magazine. It kept you on your toes, that was all. The practice manager told her she had to put the magazines out, rather than keep them back, but she used to get annoyed if a patient had got there first. She couldn't call them clients. Once she shouted at a patient because he was filling in a crossword she'd been looking forward to tackling – that stupid Maureen had put the magazine out on the table. After that they asked her, ever so politely, to leave. So now she was at home all day, looking down the garden to the road, where accidents came and happened right in front of her.

Weeks passed. No one removed the flowers, and they became windblown, sunburned, tattered. Eventually she marched down to the bottom of the garden and snipped them off the lamp-post, gathered up all the cracked cellophane and the musty stems and carried them back inside, where she put them in a plastic bag by the bin. They stayed there for a couple of days, and then she threw them out.

The next day there was a knock at her door.

'Where are my son's flowers?'

He was around her age, and he looked as if someone had hit him right in the stomach, when he least expected it. This had also once happened in the surgery. When the doctor had come up for air he looked like this man: deeply shocked, absolutely unable to believe that anyone could do that to him. Bereft, she thought afterwards, of belief. Like a crossword clue. *Eleven letters, 4, 2, 5, loss of faith.* There was something funny around his eyes, as if they could fold in on themselves.

'I buried them,' she said, quick as a flash.

'Oh,' he said, and turned back, to look down the garden. 'Oh, that's . . . that's nice. Where?'

'Down there,' she said, pointing to where the cars were roaring past. She had been digging the bed that afternoon, picking up the last of the bits of yellow plastic and broken glass.

'You buried the flowers?'

'They were dead,' she said. 'They were very tatty.' He seemed to want something more, kept looking up at her. 'I wouldn't have thrown them away, would I?'

'No. No, of course not.' He brightened, setting his shoulders back, as if she was a customer, or someone who had asked him the way. 'Burying them was the right thing to do.' He collapsed in on himself again, and she wondered whether she should offer him a cup of tea, but he was already turning back down the path.

The next day he was back again. 'Can I look?'

'What, at the garden?'

'At the spot. I didn't want to . . . you know, without telling you. And there's no pavement.'

She saw that he had no space, no public space for the mourning of his son. Just the road, a racetrack, which belongs to the council, or the government, and her lawn, her flower beds.

'Of course you can. I did bury them quite deep, you know.'

'Did you?' he said, absently. 'That's kind.'

'Well, I don't know if it was kind or not,' she began, but he was off down the bottom of the garden again.

She watched him out of her bay window, and after quarter of an hour, she brought him a cup of tea. He was simply standing there, his feet sinking into her grass, looking across the ring road. The cars flashed by him. She noticed a large piece of clear plastic or glass just a few inches from his shoes, and had to fight down the urge to pick it up in front of him. What would she say? 'These damn joy-riders. Look at the mess they leave'?

'He wasn't drunk, or anything,' he said, as if she had said it anyway. 'He was just coming home from work. Wasn't speeding. Couldn't: too much traffic. They think maybe he swerved. To avoid a cat, or something.'

'They do have cats next door. Maybe you should go there,' she said.

'Well, you know, the cat got away. He would have liked that. Can't interrogate a cat.'

'I'm not fond of them,' she said.

'Well, neither am I, overmuch.' And he smiled at her, and drank his tea, and raised his eyebrows at her through the steam from the cup.

He returned the following week.

'Just another look?' he said, and she bit back a sigh. She followed him down to the bottom of the garden, though. 'I can't,' he said, and stopped. 'I can't seem to make sense of it. He was a lovely boy. He was lovely.'

She was taken aback by this. It was the word, lovely: *six letters, pleasing passion sounds like valley*. A lovely boy. Boys were lovely: affectionate, sticky-fingered, their hair stuck up at the front, gap-toothed. Her boy had been lovely, a long time ago.

'How old was he?' she asked, unable to shake the thought of a teenage joyrider from her mind.

'Just turned thirty,' he said, and the teenager drove out of her mind, leaving this lovely boy, just turned thirty.

'Ricky. He was called Richard, but we always called him Ricky. He was married. She's called Helen. But we'll never have grandchildren now.' He knelt down, and retied his shoelace. When he stood up his knee was wet, and so was his cheek.

67

'How's his wife?' she asked, thinking that she should have used the word widow. More exact. *Ex-wife has short night behind the shutters, five letters.* Nor would she have grandchildren. Nor would she. Not from her son.

'Oh, she's heartbroken. I really mean that. Her heart is broken in pieces. It sounds like a bad song, doesn't it? She's staying with us, they're keeping her job open. I think she should go back. We've all got to go back, sooner or later. I just can't help . . . stopping here.'

'Well,' she said. 'You can stop here, any time. I really mean that.'

So he did. He would call round once a week or so, and she would make him a cup of tea, and get out biscuits, which she would buy specially. Once, she baked a cake. After the tea he would go and stand at the bottom of the garden and wander about a bit, bending down occasionally to pluck a weed from the flowerbed, or to deadhead a blown rose. They were beautiful this year, gorgeous red heads glowing up towards the house, all the way from the bottom of the garden. Sometimes he leaned against the lamp-post, which the council had straightened again. There was a big gash in the concrete, a smear of car paint. She saw him kicking at the grass one day, kicking out towards the cars zooming past him, and he said he had seen some broken glass down there. They didn't voice the thought they both had at that moment (*car eye is top light, eight letters, headlamp*), but she made him another cup of tea, and he told her again about his lovely, golden, glowing son.

He used to visit an elderly neighbour as a child and read to her, or do her shopping, and even when he'd moved into a home of his own he still wrote to her, and when he came back for Sunday lunch he'd pop round, just to check if anything needed doing. Usually it was the lawn. And his wife would do the ironing. Because she's a lovely girl too, just a lovely girl.

And the day he got his degree! He'd pretended he wasn't going to bother with all that gown and mortar board stuff: 'Silly,' he'd said. 'Not for the likes of us.' Of course, he was the first in our family to go to university. But he had, he'd kept it under his chair, and just before they called his name out he whipped it on and it was all for his mum's sake. She was crying, she was so proud. She whacked him one when we all met up again afterwards. 'Trying to kid me!' she shouted. 'You looked lovely.'

And he was a Round Tabler. Always raising money. Course, it's a way to meet friends, but I was there when he handed over the keys to a minibus for those kids, you know, the disadvantaged ones. It was fantastic, and it got into the local paper.

Dirty rag, seven letters, *tabloid*, she thought, involuntarily. But she liked the stories, which lengthened and grew until she had a vivid picture of the boy. She knew the names of his pets, and of his first girlfriend, and where he liked to drink, and what he thought of his boss. She knew that if he had had a son he would have called him Luke and, if a daughter, Megan. She knew that he really wanted to live in Tholthorpe, outside the town, but couldn't afford it yet. She knew that he smoked the odd cigarette, but that his wife didn't know about it, and that his favourite food was chicken korma. His life, straightforward in its kindnesses and its brutally simple end, nevertheless added up to an intricate pattern. A life of clues, *sail corners are overheard signs, five letters*.

She found herself drawn in, although she generally avoided difficult things. The whole of life was a puzzle to her, a series of clues to be decoded. Why should her own husband die when he had just taken out a huge loan against the business? Why should her own son turn out to be a thief, or worse? Sickening, sickening to her, that her son should be so worthless when other, more worthy boys – lovely boys, like Ricky – came to die so easily, and at the end of her garden.

In the autumn, when the glories of the rose bed had died away, he asked her if he could put a marker of some sort at the bottom of the garden. Like a memorial stone.

'You don't mean a cross, do you?' she said, although she realised she sounded suspicious.

'I was thinking of an angel,' he said. 'It could sit in the rose bed. I think it would look all right.'

'An angel. I've never had an angel in my garden.' She rather liked the idea. So he went ahead and ordered it and before Christmas it was delivered. She watched while he laid the paving stones and cemented it into place. The angel was a young girl of white marble, sitting with her legs folded away to one side, wearing a flowing robe. One hand lay in her lap, while the other reached up ('to heaven,' he said) with an outstretched forefinger. She had tiny wings, no more than fairy wings, really. On a small plaque fixed below her knees read the words: 'For Ricky, may angels guard you. Until we see you again.'

She liked that. She went down to see the angel several times a day, to read the inscription and to place a hand on the angel girl's long marble hair. It was a sign in its way, to all the drivers roaring past, that something very important had happened here. It was a clue, to the strange patterns of life.

That Christmas he invited her to spend the day with them, and she did. They had a good turkey dinner, and they played Scrabble afterwards, and she talked to Helen about

Ricky (oh, but she was looking thin), and in the afternoon they all took a trip to her house, and had a look at the angel. They liked the angel, and she felt obscurely proud, even though she knew it hadn't been her idea. She served them mince pies, *smallest secret agents sound like Christmas tarts, 5,4*, and tea, and they had a jolly time, a really jolly time. 'We like to do our bit,' said Ricky's mother, although she hadn't understood what that meant.

In the New Year he came less – still once a fortnight, but he was busier now, he said, having taken up a woodwork evening class and another in languages. It keeps me occupied, he said. It's better that way. On the other hand, Helen came quite often, spending time with the angel and the roar of the cars, and she would always come in for a cup of tea afterwards. Once she cried, about the fact she might never have children now. Never really wanted them, unless it were with Ricky. 'I thought it was all so simple,' she said. 'I had my life just like I wanted it. And now, if I want to go on, if I want it again, I mean, life, you know, start living, or something, I have to go out there.' She gestured down towards the road, to the muffled noise of the traffic. 'I've got to meet people and, oh God, I can't say this to my father-in-law, but I've got to meet someone else, do you see? I mean, fall in love with someone else. And I look at it and it looks like such hard work. So complicated.'

'Life is complicated,' she returned, thinking as she spoke, *puzzling with it? Add I'm involved, eleven letters*. 'You can only work it out one step at a time. There's no point trying to do anything more, or looking for a wider meaning, *significance of cruel marsh, seven letters*, because it's obscure, *Latin, whether second as a remedy, is dark, seven letters*. And we'll only get hurt, trying.'

The clues had been pressing in on her more lately. It was hard to hear a word without the cryptic coding rushing up to meet it in her mind. It left her breathless, unable to think very straight, although it was merely the intensifying of a pattern she had known since childhood: all things dense and complex, fighting for meaning. Now meaning itself was going, or becoming harder to detect. She was forgetting simple things, like milk – Helen started bringing her a pint every time she visited. Once, she was talking about her husband, and she forgot his name. Helen offered to do the shopping for her as well, although she couldn't remember what she'd said to that.

Her life had become simpler over the years, after her boy was sent away, after her husband passed away, after she retired from the job. It seemed hard that language should become so complicated now. She looked forward to the visits, because they brought her respite from the crowding of words, *they cut off their heads to make vocabulary, five letters*. Names could not be coded: names – Helen, Ricky – were simple, pure.

In the spring she had another visitor. He came straight up the garden, pausing for a second at the angel, and knocked hard on the door. He wore jeans, and a denim jacket, and his face was familiar, although she really couldn't place it.

'Hello, Ma. Surprised to see me?'

She made no response, for why would she be surprised to see a stranger? Or, at least, an almost stranger? *Foreigner, saint and wildlife guardian, eight letters*.

He didn't seem upset at her lack of words. He turned round, looked down the garden. 'What's that, then?' he said, pointing to the statue.

'That's for Ricky. It marks where he died. That's Ricky's angel,' she said.

She looked at him, still unable to work him out.

'Who's Ricky then?'

There was a pause.

'My son. Ricky was my son. And now he's dead.'

MAGGIE O'FARRELL

The Problem with Oliver

Fionnuala leans against the cold, salt-saturated planks of the great wooden wall that bisects the beach and pulls the cuffs of her jumper down over her hands. The sun is still bright behind the fast-moving, piled clouds but a stiff, persistent breeze is blowing off the restless, pebble-raking sea.

She looks up at the clouds: cumulo nimbus, cirro stratus, alto stratus, alto cumulus. She squeezes her eyes shut, trying to visualise that page in her geography notes. It is exactly seven and three-quarter weeks to her first A-level exam and the thought of it makes terror curdle inside her like old milk.

Fionnuala opens her eyes again and feels a momentary surprise at seeing the beach, the sky, the pebbles, the wet driftwood, and a man in a red cagoul with his trousers rolled up, hauling a yelling child after him. She glances at her watch. Four thirty. If she isn't home in twenty minutes, there will be questions about why her orchestra practice overran. Where is he?

She shifts her schoolbag to the other shoulder, her thoughts slipping sideways on to their usual track, a track that runs always parallel to whatever she's doing: if she has seven and three-quarter weeks and three subjects, that gives her roughly two weeks and three-and-a-third days for each; but if she takes one day off per week, then –

Suddenly he's there, right in front of her and he is cupping his freezing hands around her face and his lips are icy and rigid with cold and she is wrapped inside his big coat and the sea breeze is whipping her hair into his so that she can't tell whose hair is whose. And her mind has slipped sideways again but this time she is just thinking: Oliver, Oliver.

Three streets away, Grainne raises her head from her bench. She glances at the locked and bolted door of the kiln. She massages her neck with two of her knuckles, then looks out of the window. The cat is inching along the wall, body held low, eyes fixed on a finch which is pecking at some crumbs.

Grainne picks up a clay-heavy cloth and hurls it at the window. It thunks against the pane, scaring the bird into sudden, vocal flight.

The cat stares in at her, swishing its tail like a lash.

Oliver is full of excuses: he was late out of class, the bus was delayed, the traffic terrible. He doesn't go to the local school, like Fionnuala, but a private school outside South-wold.

'How long have we got?'

'Not long,' she looks at her watch and pulls a face, 'about fifteen minutes.'

He sighs and his arms loosen around her. 'Finn,' he began (when he'd first asked her name, she'd swallowed the last two syllables – it was less embarrassing and that way he could never find out that she was named for a mythological princess who was turned into a swan), 'I don't really know why we have to . . . carry on being this . . . this secretive. It seems kind of . . . weird. I mean, she can't be that bad, can she?'

This was the only disadvantage of him going to a

different, out-of-town school. Everyone at the comprehensive knew that her mother was the mad Irish potter. Heard the one about the dyslexic Irish devil-worshipper? Sold his soul to Santa. Heard the one about the Irish turkey? It was looking forward to Christmas.

Fionnuala grimaces. 'No, she is. You don't know her.' She doesn't say that her mother has a contempt for English men equalled only by her feelings towards weak tea and amoebic dystentery. She tries to joke: 'How can I tell her I've got a boyfriend called Oliver?'

He frowns, slightly hurt. 'What?'

'Well,' she says slowly. Jesus, does she have to spell it out for him? 'Irish people sometimes have a bit of a problem with that name.'

'How come?'

'You know.' Please know. 'Cromwell and all that.' She looks at his face, flushed and perplexed, close to hers. Can he really not know? Really really? Do you know nothing about history, she wants to say, nothing at all? Then hears the question, shouted, in her mother's voice. 'Never mind,' she says.

When she pushes open the front door, a familiar smell hits her: the pungent chemicals of glazing, the chalky dampness of clay. When she was little, she used to wish her house smelt like other people's – of roast dinners, fresh bread, furniture polish.

'Hello,' she shouts as she wipes her feet, seeing, in a slight panic, sand spraying up from the mat. 'Hello?'

Then her mother is coming round the door from the kitchen, her shirt studded with clots of dried clay, her arms grey to the elbows. She is laughing. 'Do you know,' she is saying, 'I just had an out of body experience!'

Fionnuala eyes her. Has she been smoking? 'What?'

'An out of body experience,' she repeats, 'my first ever. I looked out of the window and I saw you coming along the pavement and do you know for a split second I thought, what am I doing out there? Why am I walking along the road?' She laughs again, looking closely at her, as if willing Fionnuala to understand. 'And then I realised it was you, and I was me, in here, in the house.'

Fionnuala lets her bag slump to the floor. Her mother is mad. It's official. They don't even look alike – not any more. Not since Fionnuala started straightening her hair. 'What are you talking about?' she mutters, furious. 'How could you think I was you?' She pushes past her mother, into the kitchen. 'Anyway, I'm surprised you could see anything, through that stupid tree.'

The tree is a big bone of contention, not only between Fionnuala and her mother, but between her mother and the neighbours, the council, the tourist board – anyone and everyone. Her mother refuses to cut it or trim it or even touch it. Because it's a hawthorn tree and folklore has it that the fairies live in hawthorn trees and that they will wreak a terrible revenge on you if you damage their home. Irish folklore, of course.

Fionnuala once made the mistake of explaining this to a girl at school, who then told the whole class and soon people she didn't even know were shouting after her, 'How's the leprechaun tree?'

She looks out at the immense black-branched tree, which now covers their entire house, making it a tiny Sleeping Beauty's palace. 'Oh, please cut it, Mum,' she begs suddenly. 'Please. You don't even believe in fairies.'

'Do I not?' her mother says with that slow smile so that Fionnuala knows she's trying to annoy her. 'You can't underestimate them. They're not like your sissy English fairies. These are the great, indigenous tribes of Ireland who were driven underground by the invading Celts.'

'What are they doing in Suffolk, then?' Fionnuala mutters, reaching for the kettle.

'How was orchestra?' Grainne asks her daughter.

'All right,' Fionnuala bumps the kettle against the tap, making a loud clashing noise.

'What were you playing?'

'Um,' the water thunders into the metal bottom of the kettle. 'A bit of Elgar. And . . . some Britten.'

As Fionnuala turns round Grainne sees her glance towards the beach hut key, hanging on a nail beside the backdoor. The hut belongs to a friend of hers in London – Grainne keeps the key for her here.

'So,' she says, picking at the clay ingrained under her fingernails, 'do you have work to do tonight?'

'Uh-huh.' Again, Grainne sees her glance at the key, as if measuring the distance between it and her.

'Revising, is it?'

'Yeah.' Fionnuala slinks sideways and escapes from the room, forgetting the boiling kettle, which is filling the air with steam.

Fionnuala has a literature test paper spread out on her desk. She is timing herself. Her alarm clock says she's been at this forty-five minutes but she's only on question two. How can that be?

She hunches closer to the block of foolscap and reads the question again: *Orwell's overriding theme is the individual caught in a hostile social mechanism. Discuss.* Fionnuala sees her pen moving: *Orwell's overriding theme,* she begins. Then she stops.

Why had she said that to Oliver? That she could get the key to the beach hut for tomorrow? She must be mad. Does she want to . . . does she want *that*? She's ridiculously old not to have done it, judging by the standards of most of the people at school, but her mother has always warned her against it. Don't give them what they want, she yells, it'll save you a lot of fecking trouble later on. Grainne had been younger than she is now when she'd had her and had to move to England to get away from the fury of her family.

'Fionnuala!' The sound of her mother's voice knifing into the silence makes her jump. 'Dinner!'

In the kitchen, her mother is dropping ripped, damp lettuce leaves on to two plates. Fionnuala seizes her left wrist. 'For Chrissake, Mum, you could have washed your hands.' Everything her mother cooks tastes of clay.

'Sorry, love. Forgot.' She splits the baked potatoes in two and slaps a yellow wedge of butter into their pale, steaming innards. 'Want to see what I made today?'

'OK,' Fionnuala says grudgingly, picking up the plates.

In the studio, Grainne uncovers a tray of Celtic crosses, wall plaques, paperweights, keyfobs, pendants. Her daughter looks them over, expressionless, forking potato into her mouth.

'The usual shite for the Yanks and the Brits,' Grainne says. 'Eiresatz – it keeps a roof over our head.' She whips the cover off the second tray: deep-sided bowls, curved like boat hulks, swarming with tiny three-dimensional figures. When Fionnuala was a child, she'd loved Grainne's chunky, faceless homunculi. Grainne made her an entire house of them, complete with their own minuscule beds, cups, plates

79

and bath. Grainne wonders for a moment where it got to. Must be in the attic somewhere.

Fionnuala stretches out a finger and touches two embracing figures, poised on the circular brink of a bowl. Grainne watches her. Sometimes Fionnuala is so like she was at that age it makes Grainne suspicious that someone somewhere is playing a joke on them, making time loop round twice.

'I like them,' her daughter says, removing her hand. 'Will you sell them?'

'Don't know yet.' Grainne gets up quickly, covering the paperweights. Fionnuala wanders out of the room. Before Grainne covers the bowls, she touches the embracing figures herself, once, and very lightly, finding a place where the imprint of her own thumb lies.

Fionnuala stands in the kitchen, aghast. The key is gone. The hook where it hangs, where it always hangs, is empty. There's even a whitish shadow of the key on the wallpaper, like a photo negative.

Fionnuala puts down her plate with a crash. Her pulse is clicking painfully in her neck. *Her mother*. Her bloody mother. How does she do that? How on earth –

At the sound of her mother coming along the passage behind her, Fionnuala bolts from the kitchen, into the hall and out through the front door. She hears her mother's voice, calling: 'Where in God's name are you going?'

The night is damp and stormy, the pavements slicked with wet, the sound of the sea crashing through the gaps in the buildings. Fionnuala runs the length of their road, her breath ragged and laboured. At the lighthouse, she turns left into a narrow winding street. She yanks open the phonebox and steps in. She shivers inside her schoolshirt, the ends of her hair dripping water to the floor, to her shoulders, to the phone as she dials. Fury, or the cold, is making her shake so that she can't seem to hit the right numbers.

'Oliver? Listen, it's all off. Tomorrow's off. She knows.'

Back at the house, the windows are all burning with light. Fionnuala kicks off her sodden shoes at the door and thuds up the stairs, into her room. She knows she needs to sink on to her bed and cry – she just needs to. But as her body hits the crochetted cover her mother made her when she was a baby, she feels the hard crinkle of paper.

Fionnuala shifts her weight, pushing the damp skeins of hair away from her eyes. It's an envelope. Red, squarish. Her name in her mother's handwriting.

She rips it open with the edge of her finger. A brass key drops out, on to the bed. And a note: *Bring him back for tea some afternoon. I'd like to meet him. I might even make a cake.*

Fionnuala stands and goes over to the window. The house is empty, she realises, her mother gone – somewhere. She looks out into the street. The dark, twisted branches of the hawthorn tree tap-tap against the side of the house, as if wanting to come in.

LISA SABBAGE

Elvis and the Mermaid

T HE FILLINGS in their teeth shook and rattled, but no
one spoke or even shifted their gaze. There was nothing unusual in this. It was the same every lunchtime. They
came to escape their office jobs, to gather at the rim of the
construction site, peer down at the dusty figures below, and
to watch their dirty bodies shudder in tandem with the
jackhammers disemboweling the aged building.

Elvis was glad of the noise. He did not want to talk. He
was there to feel the vibrations enter his feet, move up his
legs, through his arse, and thump inside his chest, reminding
him of his own heart marking time.

Still, when the stranger nearest him glanced at his watch
and walked away, throwing down the last of his sandwich,
Elvis registered the newly empty space a little sadly and felt
his plump, downy tummy rumble mournfully. He was
trying to lose weight and, for a moment, he was tempted
to retrieve the crust from the ground and suck on it like a
teething baby.

Instead, he concentrated even harder on the wreckage
below, sighing because he longed to be down there, wearing
a hard hat and shifting the gearstick of the digger with a
satisfying metallic kick. He knew it was time to head back
to the office, but there was something compelling about
all that heavy equipment, the way it pounded at the earth,

ack-ack-ack, thunk-thunk-thunk, as if to say let me in, let me in. It was a seduction of sorts, this oddly familiar, soothing rhythm that seeped up from the ground to lick and suck at him. He felt comforted, becalmed by the workers in their colour-coded vests, hauling order out of disorder, creating a monolith that would stand forever.

Except it wouldn't, would it, thought Elvis. One day it would fall, just like the sphinx succumbing to syphilitic sands.

Hearing a police siren in the distance, he felt sufficiently guilty to finally tear himself away. But, before he turned and crossed the road, he allowed himself one quick glance to check if the mermaid had come.

He thought of her as the mermaid because of the coat she had been wearing that first morning he had seen her at the bus stop, politely letting others board before her, singular and shimmering in the mysterious garment which seemed to tremble green and blue.

After that, sitting on the bus they shared almost every day, he had kept watch for her, noting that her hair was often wet, as if she had come fresh from the sea, and, that at some point in each journey, she would fish into her handbag and retrieve delicate chocolates wrapped in gem-coloured cellophane and foil. He looked forward to it, this sharing of moments, even if the mermaid was unaware they were shared.

Strange how, even in a big city like this one, some faces become familiar. He had soon spotted her in other places, too. On the street, in the cafés where he bought his lunch, and here at the building site.

Just not today, he sighed, consoling himself by kicking an empty can along the gutter.

It was a childish thing to do, thought the mermaid,

unseen but observant none the less. He certainly resembled a child, this man from the bus, with his doughnut face, his red hair, and his ill-fitting suit.

In fact, now that she thought about it, he resembled a long-ago classmate, a boy she had sat alongside for a whole year, unremarkable apart from his clumsy habit of dropping things. She had dismissed that boy as stupid, maybe even backward, until a friend informed her that he was actually down on his knees looking up her skirt.

At the time, she had not understood the logic of this. Why go to all that trouble when every playtime she and the other girls engaged in a ritualistic knicker display, hanging upside down from the climbing frames or exploding into cartwheels? Now she realised that he had been interested in something else altogether, that the cave of desks and shadows between skirt and thigh suggested other places and other rituals.

Elvis had not been this kind of boy. He had been more concerned with dinosaurs and fossils and archaeology. At times he still found himself daydreaming about the ancient Greeks and Romans, imagining himself as Odysseus tacking into an unknown world.

Maybe that was why he had noticed the mermaid.

Dawdling back to work, he tried to picture her floating on a bank of water and wondered whether she was as thin and penumbral as he imagined her to be. Or perhaps she would have hidden strength stripped into her bone and muscle. He chewed his lip: the one thing he was certain of was that she would recoil from the big bloated mass of his own body.

At some distance behind him, the mermaid was trailing Elvis, trying to keep track of his red hair as it flashed in the murky stream of pedestrians. Indeed, she was so intent upon the task that, like a child, she had crossed the road without checking for traffic. Sorry, she mouthed at the irritated driver who had braked and leant on his horn, and by the time she reached the other side, Elvis had vanished.

Elvis did not turn back to see where the noise had come from. As he neared his own workplace, his tummy rumbled for the second or maybe third time. Oh well, he thought, only three and a half more hours to go. Two hundred and ten minutes. Twelve thousand, six hundred seconds. Maybe he'd burn a few extra calories by walking faster.

He picked up his pace for a bit, then, realising it would only mean spending more time at work, he slowed down again.

No one would miss him anyway, he thought, smiling ruefully. Because he was fat, people looked the other way. Affronted by his bulk, they tried to pretend they could not see him. And you could not miss an invisible man.

Sure enough, none of his colleagues so much as glanced up when he ambled down the corridor. No one demanded to know where he'd been or what he thought he was doing. No one came in and asked him to account for himself as he squeezed back into his chair and tried to focus on the spreadsheet in front of him. It was just as well. How could he explain that the columns of numbers kept turning into the pillars of the building site, sprouting reinforced steel like veins in a severed arm?

He tapped his pen on his thigh, undid his top button, and leaned back in his chair, recalling the controversy before the contractors had begun tearing down the old arcade. He had a newspaper clipping somewhere, a report about the old fogies who had picketed and protested, claiming the dark Victorian edifice with its ornate cornices and stone was worth preserving. There was even a sit-in, he remembered. But in the end the machines and the men who operated them had crept in and started work in the middle of the night, like the monsters that sneak under children's beds as soon as the lights are turned off.

Clever, thought Elvis.

Still he felt some sympathy with the protestors. There was something about stone. It suggested history, even where none existed. It implied stability and permanence, the very things that cities with all their flux and constant change lack most.

Now a straight-backed tower of steel and glass was replacing the lazy, slouching stone. The curvature of the old building would become lines and angles. Exclamations would take the place of speech marks. A new smooth and flawless surface would reflect the future back at passers by, who would wonder at the light and space displayed behind the glass wall, no less a wall for being glass.

'Afternoon tea Elvis,' one of his colleagues announced, all thin and sprightly and bounding along the corridor on his way to the canteen.

It was the first thing anyone had said to him all day.

The emptiness gripped at his stomach as he opened his desk drawer and took out an apple. God, what he'd do for some decent food, he grimaced, biting into its soft, floury flesh.

Chewing slowly and looking out his window at the office tower opposite, he recalled that anorexics often dream of glass coffins.

Not so far away, the mermaid was standing outside and unwrapping yet another chocolate, gripping its golden wrapper between her fingers, and trying to ignore the dull ache behind her eyes.

'Have lips,' she sang to herself, 'will kiss . . .'

She coughed, her throat tightening around some piece of grit or ash riding on the dirty air.

'Have love, to share. With you-ou-ou-ou-ou, in the tunnel of love.'

She carried on humming for a while, trying to remember the words and thinking how temperamental the city was.

Sometimes, when the wind blew along the canyons of tarmac and tower buildings, she felt as if she might fly away unnoticed.

'And if you do, then I'll give you . . .'

On autumn afternoons, stepping out into the pearly light after the rain, the streets appeared like rivers of mercury, beautiful but poisonous, crowded with bodies that pushed and bruised her until she wanted to weep.

'Everything I've got.'

Yet on late evenings, after those same streets had emptied out, their glacial aridity could fill her with so much joy that she would shout just to hear her voice echo back like the greeting between the last two people on earth.

At times, she wanted to share it with nobody. At others, she despaired that no one would ever save her from it.

Savouring the last tiny sliver of chocolate, she placed the neatly folded wrapper in her handbag and dragged herself back into the confines of the building.

In the bathroom, she splashed water on her face and searched in the mirror. At the corners of her eyes, she could see more lines appearing, as if the fabric of her skin would unravel if she pulled at the threads.

As she patted away the last few drops of moisture, the door swung open violently and two of the sales and marketing lot came clattering in. 'Oh hello . . .' one of them said, clearly unable to remember her name.

She managed a quick smile, but her stomach churned when she heard them erupt into sharp giggles behind her.

It was as if all her nightmares were coming true and she was vanishing into the walls and alleyways, seeping down between the cracks in the pavement.

She resisted the urge to run, placing one foot carefully in front of the other until she came to her desk. I will not disappear, she told herself. I am flesh and blood and bone and marrow.

Somehow, she tethered herself there until the clock finally snailed its way around to 5.30 and she was free again, with her chocolates and her handbag and her fears.

Lighting a cigarette, she made her way to the building site. She wasn't ready to go home just yet and she stopped for a while, throwing the spent butt into the chasm and watching it bounce and tumble away. It was much quieter now. There was no red-haired man and no crowd of strangers. The machinery was dormant and there were only a few on-site stragglers, dusting off the last tasks of their day. She watched, fascinated, as a solitary worker knelt on a plank of wood and slid backwards across a pond of rough, wet concrete, using a trowel to smooth the trail he left in front of him. This struck her as quietly amusing. It was the opposite of a life in which you were supposed to clear your path as you go, not after you've been, all traces obliterated, as if you had never been there at all.

Elvis did not see the mermaid on the bus that night, or the next. He wasn't unduly worried. He imagined her surfacing for a while then slipping back beneath the water. He had learned to be patient.

He kept watch and stuck to his diet. He counted calories, he went for low fat and high fibre, eschewed roasts for grills, fried for steamed, plump for lean. Nothing seemed to help. He still looked like Billy Bunter. He still dreamed of chocolate, and fried chicken and double helpings of lasagne, and he still dawdled back to his office after gazing at the construction site. Occasionally he let himself imagine how the absent mermaid's long, slender fingers would feel on his warm, clammy skin if he were to stand beside her and reach for her hand. But she was beautiful, he thought, and she would no doubt recoil back into her ocean of grace.

In the shower at night, he tried to ignore the soft, flaccid curves of his body, thinking instead of the lean, hard lines of the building. It was beginning to resemble a huge labyrinth and this troubled Elvis. There was no discernible pattern. He could not decide where one room started and where another ended and became a corridor. It was full of strange tunnels that led nowhere, of ceilings that contained no floors.

Where was the order, wondered Elvis as he blinked behind the metal grating that kept him and all the other strangers from slipping in.

The mermaid too, wondered about the building and its power over the grown men and women who contemplated it. They reminded her of children at the beach who gather to stare at rotting fish and the other detritus of death washed up on every tide.

She went there now only to look for the red-haired man. She could see he was fat, no question. But not unpleasantly so. She found him whole and rounded. Bountiful. He reassured her. He was weighty and rooted. A strong wind would not blow him away. He would make a good and solid anchor. If asked.

The truth was, she would have avoided the place altogether if not for him. There is a moment in the life of every building when it becomes unclear whether it is going up or coming down; the form is so shaky, so interrupted and undefined that its destiny appears to hang in the balance. If rain or bad weather halt construction even for a day or two, entropy quickly sets in. The scaffolding begins to look tired, the materials take on the air of abandoned neglect, warping, splitting, or crumbling too soon. Tarpaulin and sheets of plastic, thrown down hastily to protect vulnerable details, seem scruffy and dishevelled, even vaguely distasteful like the soiled clothes of the wino or junkie.

The mermaid could not help noticing that rubbish was now accumulating around the edges of the site, as if it was a vacuum drawing everything into its hollow core. It had assumed an unhealthy pallor, the whiff of piss and violence, and a general grubbiness that made her want to wash her face and hands in hot, soapy water.

It depressed her.

All these people, she thought, all these people staring in, inhaling the cement mix and dust, passively watching the sky divided and blocked out.

Once or twice she spotted him, but he was always on the far side of the site, too distant to do anything but wave. And of course she could not wave because they did not know each other.

She cleared her throat to sing, but changed her mind.

When Elvis finally saw her again, it was a muggy, drizzly morning and he was tired and in pain because his fingers had swollen into tight little sausages in the humidity. He was running late and the bus was so full that he was forced to stand among the other awkward, perspiring commuters. His skin immediately began to creep. He was afraid people would notice how profusely he was sweating, but he couldn't wipe his palms without drawing attention to himself. It was a sickening dilemma and he began to panic.

At the next stop, desperate for space and air, he decided to jump off and wait for another, emptier bus.

Then he saw the mermaid.

The doors swung open and there she was. Embarrassed, he retreated as she stepped toward him in her opalescent coat. For an instant, as she looked around for something to hold on to, their eyes met and he was sure he saw a flash of recognition and the beginning of a smile. But she had dropped her umbrella and bent down to retrieve it and, when she straightened up again, she had turned her back to him. He did notice, though, that her hair smelled faintly of chocolate and caramel.

When the bus finally reached the last stop and they had all spilled out into the city streets, he briefly considered catching up with her. But he soon lost his nerve. He hated the way women always flinched when he told them his name was Elvis. And anyway, he thought, he didn't want to frighten her with his clumsiness and his bulk.

The mermaid herself slid away, feeling unsafe in the wake of the inexplicable desire that had washed over her, the desire to clasp her arms around his waist and steady herself.

She dreamt of him that night, a nightmare in which he had become limbless and faceless. She kept trying to ask him what was wrong, but nothing came out of her mouth. And, at seven the next morning when her alarm went off, she phoned in sick. She felt frightened.

Elvis ran a bath and lay in the water for an hour, watching the fat on his chest float like breasts. He cupped them in his hands, growing angry at the weight of them and the strange lie his body seemed to be telling him. The laxatives were kicking in now and he sat on the toilet and shat for fifteen minutes, shat as if he was shitting the very life out of himself. He shivered, dried himself quickly and dressed, not even daring to look in the mirror before he left and locked the door behind him.

He walked with his head down and did not crane his neck to search for the mermaid, who was probably stupid anyway. He did not pause at the building site, and he made it to work in plenty of time. At lunch, he stayed at his desk, working on figures and chewing his apple and salad with disinterest. He overheard someone talking about the building, but he didn't care. It was just a fucking building, he thought, it would go up, it would come down. The glass and steel would become smeared and caked in birdshit. It would grow old and neglected and become an embarrassment, a memory that everyone would rather forget.

After work, he took a different bus route home.

The next day they both felt guilty. The mermaid felt guilty because she hadn't really been sick, she had just been tired and unnerved. She had spent the entire day in bed, dozing and watching television. Which made her feel even more afraid and in danger of vanishing nameless and unremembered. Elvis felt guilty because he had thought such horrible things about himself, the building and even the mermaid. It was like all his hunger was eating away at his heart, not his flesh.

On the bus he hid behind his newspaper and did not look up when the mermaid got on. He did not see her take out a new box of chocolates, carefully undoing its golden ribbon. Nor did he see that her hair was dry or that she had smiled in his direction.

By the time she reached work, the mermaid felt sick to her stomach, kneading her hands to reassure herself that her skin contained mass, that she was flesh and blood and could not be absorbed into the walls and foundations.

During his lunch hour, Elvis went for a brisk walk before pausing at the building site. He ignored the growling in his gut as he spooned low-fat yoghurt into his mouth and was just about to resume his walk when he heard a scream. It was a woman's scream and it startled him.

Searching for its source, he noticed a small crowd gathering at the far corner of the building site, huddling against the railing and pointing at a spot he could not see.

It was only then that he began to panic, began to move his legs without realising he was moving them. It was only then that he knew something was wrong with him, knew that the hollow space gnawing inside him had nothing to do with the diet or the laxatives.

By the time he reached the murmuring crowd, a siren was wailing up from the site and the workers had downed their tools.

Oh God, thought Elvis, oh God, oh God.

Desperate now to see what he feared most, he pushed his way through the clump of shocked onlookers. Breathing heavily and gripping the metal fence, he stared down, waiting for the force of it to hit him. But still his vision was obscured, this time by the knot of workers bending into the platform where the body lay.

'God,' he said, fearing that the earth had already swallowed her up and that he would have to jump in after her.

'Can you see who it is?' he asked no one in particular.

'Can you see?' he said again.

But still no one answered.

Then, one by one, the site workers moved back from their serried centre like the petals of a flower opening, and Elvis saw the form, lying crumpled and insensible. The wall of his heart buckled but held, and he shuddered and felt his whole body go slack with relief. It was not the mermaid.

It's him, she blinked. That body, that faraway broken body, belonged to the solitary worker she had observed levelling the concrete into a perfect plane.

Drawn irrevocably closer, she was shocked to see the red-haired man pressed against the fence. It was not so much the clarity of the strawberry freckles and soft red hairs on his skin, but the tenderness in his face, and the way the crowd thinned out around him, leaving him there pinned and wriggling on his emotion.

Maybe he knew the man, too, she thought, before realising her mistake: she had not really known the man at all.

Then an odd thing happened. Standing at the verge of the site in the midst of a crowd she did not like or understand, she realised that she did not have to be ruled by towers and minarets, that she did not have to wait to be saved.

Stuff it, she thought.

Elvis did not know how long he had been standing there when he finally relaxed his grip on the fence. As he examined the grey marks the metal had left in his palms, his belly growled with hunger. Christ, he thought, what kind of a man am I?

He was wiping his eyes when he felt a tap on his shoulder and automatically shifted aside to make room for another onlooker.

'Excuse me,' someone said, touching his arm again.

This time Elvis looked up. First, he registered the blue and green coat, then that her eyes were not the blue he had imagined, but a rich deep brown. Then he saw that the mermaid was holding out her hand. To him.

Smiling, she unfolded her fingers to reveal layers of

turquoise cellophane that seemed to glitter and dance in her palm like some ancient, magical treasure.

'Hello,' she said, 'my name's Rapunzel.'

Below them, astonishing all witnesses to his fall, the injured man suddenly opened his eyes and began to laugh.

VALERIE THORNTON

Or Maybe Gold

T HE FIRST problem was solved easily enough with the arrival of the community service boys and their buckets of brown paint.

'Da!' the boy shouted. 'They're at it again!'

He looked down from the second floor window and watched his da's images being obliterated from the long strip of wall bordering the football pitch. The plaintive mewing of his new wee sister came from the back room.

'See, son – it's a compliment really. It means they've noticed it. The less time it lasts, the bigger the compliment. It was a good send-off, but.'

The boy watched as his da's flamboyant black and silver representation of a train, with a smiling coffin floating in a cloud above the driver, was brushed away. The sweeping horizontal lines of the carriages were distinctively his and the serenity he'd achieved was comforting for the whole family. It had been a commemoration wall for his Uncle Kasso who'd spent his life working on the trains, emblazoning their carriages with swathes of colour and dramatic patterns of secret lettering, legible only to other artists.

The train, whose roof he had been decorating last week – a twenty-first birthday train for a mate – had unexpectedly started and he'd fallen under the wheels and been crushed. Auntie Ariane hadn't stopped crying since.

'Such a shame for your ma too,' Otto said, 'but her brother, your Uncle Kasso, was a great artist and will never be forgotten. A clever man too. Managed to get away from school without the taint of a single standard grade. Not many folk can achieve that!'

'He'll no see ma new wee sister now,' the boy said.

'No, son. I'll have to put a real special birth painting there for the bairn, won't I? There goes my sign.'

They watched as the smiling face that was Otto's mark – a pupil in the centre of each of the 'O's, the two 't's for the nose, a smile curved below, and the whole enclosed in an almost complete circle of bright red capital G – was extinguished by darkness as if it had never existed.

'Tell me again,' Otto said. 'I want to know you'll always remember.'

'G Otto: he was an Italian, a long time ago who painted on walls nearly as well as you do.'

'Well done, lad!' Otto scruffed up his son's dark hair with his good left hand.

The second problem was going to be more difficult to solve.

'How're you going to do Hayley's birth painting now?' the boy asked.

Otto looked wryly at the stookie on his right arm, his spraying arm.

'Bad timing, wasn't it, son? At least I'll no have to change nappies for a bit. Maybe you will!'

The boy was for ever getting into trouble at school for covering his jotters with pictures and stylised lettering. Maybe it was because he himself was tall and thin, but he was especially fond of margins, those long slim rectangles of blank space which spoke to him of the connection between the skies and the earth. He would draw the little world in the bottom few lines of the page and fill the heaven space above with moons and suns, stars and winged creatures, some human, some animal. Then he would get a bawling out from the teacher for ruining yet another jotter.

He aspired to decorate the close mouths all round Patrick. He loved those beautiful vertical stones which defined the entrances, and he looked up longingly at the unreachable pairs of red sandstone pillars which held up each and every bay window in the burgh. But there was a strict code of honour: you didn't do folks' homes.

When he grew up, he wanted to be an artist like his da and uncle. He wanted to get commissions for wall work too, for new babies, weddings, funerals or any other surprise celebration. He wanted to work under cover of darkness and illuminate the world his patrons would waken up to, with colours and images and words which would flare briefly and burn into the memory of all who saw it. He wanted to be paid, like them, in food and drink and clothes and goodwill.

He still remembered the delight on the faces of his aunt and uncle when his da had taken them on a surprise walk on their wedding day last year, down to the entrance to the cycle track under the expressway.

He'd got together with his mates and they'd lined the underpass with celebratory images – roses, champagne, hearts and horseshoes and the happy couple holding hands under sunshine and blue skies without even a hint of the cloud that had now descended on his aunt with the loss of her man. He'd been allowed to paint the lucky black cat crossing their path, and he wondered if maybe it was somehow all his fault because he hadn't been good enough to paint luck properly.

He would have to do a painting to make her feel happy again, as well as to welcome wee Hayley and make his ma, who'd lost her brother, smile, and his da feel better about his broken arm.

'Can I stay with Auntie Ariane tonight?'

'That's a nice idea, son. You'll be a comfort to her. But no nonsense, mind!'

He went down to her landing and chapped the door. He'd changed into dark clothes, which she might take as a mark of respect. His bedroom was above hers, and he had heard her weeping gently through the nights for her lost man.

'Ma wee lad!' she said, hugging him fit to crush the breath out of him. Her hair smelt old and sad. She turned away weeping, holding a tissue to her watery eyes, her face bloated with grief. He thought she looked really quite scary like this but because he knew her well, he wasn't afraid.

'I'm sorry, son. I miss him so much. I just can't believe I'll no see him again.'

He let her sip coffee and talk about Kasso, her beloved Kasso. He was waiting for it to grow dark. And all the time he was doodling up the margins of her unread Evening Times, seeing it in his head.

'You should've seen what he did on the coast train when you were born, son. He and I were sweethearts even then,' she paused to pull another tissue from the box at her elbow and hold it to her eyes. 'He wasn't called P Kasso for nothing. What a welcome you had into the world and everyone from here to Helensburgh and back again could see it for days. D'you know, son, I don't think there is a square inch of his work left. Not anywhere. And he must have painted acres. I've got his drawings here but, and all his paints.'

It was the opportunity he'd been waiting for.

'Could I get some, please, Auntie Ariane? For ma da,' he added quickly.

'Any time, son. Kasso would've been happy for him to have them.'

'Now?'

'Eh?' For the first time she looked directly at him.

'Can I get them now? The cans?'

'Oh. Aye. OK, son.'

He knew exactly what he wanted and piled them into a Safeway bag, his heart thumping at the excitement of it all.

'Right, I'd better be getting up the stairs.'

'Bless you, son. Mind how you go and keep away from trains, whatever you do, pet.'

The boy went upstairs and waited at his own door until he heard Auntie Ariane close her door for the night. The sound of Hayley's thin wail trailed through the painted glass panel towards him. He turned and tiptoed down to the back court.

He sat and waited by the bin shelter, the smell of rotting oranges and old bones dampened by the cool of the evening. The black and white feral cat stopped in its tracks, stared unblinking at him and then scuttled past, tail down, belly to the ground, and into the bin shelter to rustle through the rubbish.

He looked up at his own backroom window where the pink curtains glowed warmly. His ma was behind them, in there with Hayley. He felt shut out. He hadn't seen his ma properly for days now. She was too busy with the baby. He missed most being hugged, and the way her long dark hair, which smelt of roses, would swing around him like a cape of love.

He was cold and stiff by the time the last bedroom and bathroom lights in the close were extinguished, though he'd kept his hands under his oxters to keep them warm. The half moon was high above the chimney pots as he crept through the close, careful not to let the front door bang.

It was the first time he'd done it for real, with proper cans, on a proper wall. He knew he had to work quickly and that he had to keep the jet spray of colour moving to avoid the drips that characterised an amateur.

But he knew exactly what he was going to do, and it was as if his hand had done it many times before, in another life. And, for the very first time, he could use his own sign.

Like all great artists who work in the dark, he'd already learned to tell the colour by its smell: black smelt of soot; yellow had a bright acidic smell; red was mellow and strong; blue had a thin, light smell; green was bright and sweet; and white had no smell but made him breathe more slowly. Gold and silver were the only two he could not distinguish. Both smelt coppery and, under the yellow streetlight, looked identical. He would risk golden stars and a silver sun.

He shook up the cans as quietly as he could, muffling their rattle under his dark sweatshirt, then quickly painted his Uncle Kasso in a blue heaven, with silver, or maybe gold, stars and a moon. He was beaming love down in long lines from his fingertips to the earth far below him, and wee new Hayley was bathed in a cone of golden, or maybe silver, light. Quickly he painted a woman with weeping eyes being comforted in another cone of love. He put himself on to the wall, cuddling the feral cat which was no longer afraid of him. It had a gift smile on its face for Hayley. Behind him, with her arm around him, his ma with roses in her long glittering hair, and his da with no stookie. All the lines were upward, with the great distance between heaven and earth connected by his uncle's love.

Then, in his own special script of tall thin letters, weaving in and out of each other until they were more pattern than words, he wrote in Kasso's heaven: Hello Hayley.

Finally, he flourished his sign, the sign his da had said would be his for always. A great big star high up in the sky with a long tail streaming behind it, which he dashed off with trails of both gold and silver.

'Tell me again, so I know you'll never forget, son,' his da had said.

'G A Comety: an Italian artist, who reached up to the sky because his ma was a comet with long shining hair and his da was G Otto.'

'That'll do just nicely, son. Well done!'

HILARY PLEWS

Victoria

I AVERAGED ABOUT thirty-five minutes per day in Victoria (it was eighteen minutes under British Rail). I used to spend this time thinking about which specimen to order next for my lepidoptera collection. That was before the advent of the girl.

Despite having spent twenty-five years commuting through the station, I never really noticed the details. It was just one of those grimy corridors linking home with work. Coffee was plentiful and the flower seller cunningly situated to remind me about forgotten birthdays and wedding anniversaries. After I spotted the girl (she actually lived there you see), I began to drink the place in. There are currently thirty-three outlets at which coffee is sold and you can eat every kind of fast food, but there are no serious vegetables like cabbage or turnips. I worried about vitamin deficiency. Fruit was plentiful but extremely expensive. There was no shortage of chocolate or underwear, but nothing much in the overwear department. I wondered how the girl managed to look so well turned out. No nose rings or matted rats tails for hair. No tattered jeans or trailing mongrel. Her complexion was good so she obviously enjoyed a well balanced diet. At first I supposed that she just chose well from paying customers' left-overs. Later I realised that her existence was a much more complex series of bargains and manoeuvres.

I first heard about the girl around the time I was nego-
tiating with a dealer to acquire a rare white bandit butterfly,
so called because of the black to butterscotch band of
colour bisecting the otherwise pristine white of its upper
wings. Two fellow commuters on what can now only rather
loosely be called the 8.11 to Bognor, via Croydon, were
chatting about her.

'Been living in the station for months.'

'Extraordinary. She looks quite normal. Why don't the
police or the immigration get rid of her?'

'I'm not sure if they even know about her. She doesn't
stand out in a crowd.'

'Still. You'd think someone would tell the authorities.'

'Why bother? She's never asked me for any money
although I've bought her meals and the odd bottle of Dior,
the kind of thing my daughter likes. She's a delightful girl.
Knows her stuff too.'

I was intrigued. Besides, the negotiations had stalled. I
didn't think it was correct to pay nearly one hundred
pounds for a specimen whose wingspan did not measure
a full four inches.

When I next walked through the station I began to look
about me. I noticed how all Connex South East personnel
disappeared whenever the loud speaker imparted particularly bad news about the state of the train service. I became
adept at spotting those abrupt blue uniforms as they re-
emerged from their hiding places and attempted to mingle
nonchalantly with the fare-paying public once again. I
could tell by the set of their shoulders and the length of
their stride just which service-bereft travellers were going to
complain, and how loudly and rudely. Personally, I see little
point in such complaints. In the past, before disruption
became routine, I have politely asked for written confirma-

tion of the loud speaker announcement, in order to prove the source of my late arrival to my superiors.

I was surprised by how agreeable my surroundings actually were. The hard, dropping-encrusted roof over the concourse kept out rain as well as harmful ultra violet rays. It reminded me of the impenetable cocoon made by the Puss moth caterpillar to repel aerial attack. The numerous exits meant there was a constant supply of fresh air, and the vastness of the space that comprised the concourse, including the upstairs food hall area, offered a generous exercise circuit. It occurred to me that the food gallery would also provide excellent larval feeding grounds if only the retail staff could be encouraged to convert their waste pimento and sweet corn tins into flower pots for nasturtium, sedum and buddleia.

It was six weeks after that overheard train conversation before I found her. The secret of her success was her adaptability. She had developed the art of butterfly camouflage and so looked like every other young, serious-minded female commuter. She wore a black suit and a large black shoulder bag. She was of an average height and weight, had sooty blonde hair which she wore swept back from her forehead in a ponytail, the ends of which mimicked the elongated wings of the Swallowtail. She often wore one item of clothing that matched the aggressive Connex blue. It might be a scarf or her tights or the ruff round her ponytail. She was attractive. I first spotted her standing in front of the ticket offices, mingling with the crowds waiting for their trains to appear on the electronic destination guide above their heads. Only the sharpest-eyed birds can distinguish a hibernating Comma butterfly from a tattered leaf. The average commuter would have been unable to pick her out, but *I* noticed her, because she did not look up once in the entire fifteen minutes that I stood and observed her from the side of Smith's. Genuine passengers check the destination board about once every three point six minutes in my experience. I stole closer to memorise her for identification purposes. I noticed that her cherry red lips were bracketed by two charming dimples and located within a heart shaped face. Every few minutes she would stop pacing to converse with a passenger.

I found it difficult to concentrate at work that day and I became irritable when I arrived back at Victoria in the evening and was unable to locate her. The following morning she was still nowhere to be seen. I was later to work than the absence of a train driver for the 8.11 justified. On the return journey, I divided up the concourse into quarters, and thoroughly searched each one. The movements of Connex staff confused me, as when I had last seen her, the girl had been wearing a scarf that precisely matched the vigorous blue of their uniforms. I finally found her eating dinner with an older man in the Pizza Hut in the upstairs food hall. I stayed until they finished and I noticed that the man paid, leaving a generous tip. The waiter winked at the girl as she left. I trailed the pair of them down the escalator back on to the main concourse where they walked towards the external tube steps. The girl stopped just short of the exit threshold and the man stooped to kiss her on the cheek. She then waved goodbye and turned round rather sharply. I pulled up in surprise as I had expected the girl to accompany the man home. I stepped smartly into the music shop to avoid her noticing me, and by the time I emerged, her unremarkable presence had been swallowed up by the crowd.

My time-keeping became quite erratic until I got used to the girl's movements. This caused my superiors to place a first written warning on my personnel file. I asked my wife to deal with her complaints in a similar way, but she found my suggestion inapposite.

On Tuesdays and Thursdays the girl operated from the concourse adjacent to the one on which I had first sighted her, and this disrupted my observations for several weeks. The evenings were unpredictable. She could be found enjoying her evening meal with various older men, or chatting with Connex employees or with retail outlet staff. Occasionally I saw her helping the concourse cleaners, picking up the discarded burger boxes and chocolate wrappers of those members of the public – the great majority in my view – who cannot bring themselves to flatten their refuse by folding it into a series of diminishing squares, in order to transport it home for ultimate disposal.

I was dismayed to find that mounting my latest acquisitions on clear glass rods, so as to give the impression of flight, before sealing them into air-tight acrylic cases was no longer as satisfying as it once had been. I therefore began spending most of my weekends at the station in order to watch the girl. By this stage I felt protective both of her and her habitat. I found myself directing drunks and derelicts out into the open air or back down into the underground. I repositioned the pick-and-mix stall and the beigel stand when new staff came to set them up, unaware of custom and practice. My exertions were repaid when the girl noticed me and flashed her rarely-utilised but quite dazzling and dimpled, ruby smile. I felt as excited as the day I procured the protected sooty blond Parnassus apollo with its four cherry red spots dotted across the lower wings. I bought her a caffé latte. She persuaded me to try it. I found that sticking my mouth and nose into a long glass full of hot, frothy milk flavoured with coffee misted up my spectacles. She spoke

English well but with a heavy Eastern European accent. She was shy and tended not to look directly at me when I spoke. On that first date with her, she was wearing a short black dress, with Connex blue tights, and high heeled shoes. I was surprised by how dark her eyes were. I had assumed they would be as startlingly blue as the upperside of the Adonis. I found, by the time she had drunk her coffee, thanked me and left, that I had done most of the talking. I told her about my butterfly collection, my daily commute, and how much I enjoyed doing voluntary work at Victoria. I even told her that I was thinking of leaving my wife. She told me nothing, not even her name. I hung around for a few more hours, but the girl had gone. She did not reappear on Sunday and I had to content myself with directing lost tourists. I was bothered by vivid blue Connex sightings. Sometimes these belonged to station personnel and sometimes I was left with the impression that the girl was being deliberately elusive.

After a final written warning, I took voluntary redundancy in order to spend all my time in the field. I began to understand the girl's methods. She was an excellent mimic – an unusual trait in humans. Her skill echoed the near-perfect mimicry employed by the Viceroy butterfly to pass itself off as the poison-filled Monarch. She could simulate both a fellow-traveller *and* someone with accurate information. She talked to disgruntled commuters, found out where they were going and told them what time the next train would depart, from which platform, how long the revised journey would take and failing that, gave them precise directions for getting to their destination by an alternative route. People responded warmly to her whereas they would probably have hit a Connex employee. They realised instinctively that she was not Connex, but the single item of assertive blue that she always wore was enough for them to be convinced of both her authority and her innocence. Her camouflage was complete.

She spent weekday evenings dining with different elderly men who talked while she listened. They paid and I always felt jealous. I only once saw her receive money. It was in Accessorize. The Saturday man handed over a large wad of notes. I asked her about this at our weekly lovers' meeting in Coffee Republic. She laughed saying she had earned it by stealing back from shoppers what they had lifted. When I looked concerned, and asked if this wasn't rather dangerous, and shouldn't I call the police, she stroked my hand and told me that she could look after herself.

After I moved permanently to the station, I pieced most of her story together. Her mother had been murdered by the Mafia and she had fled here to seek asylum. She was from Khatanga in Siberia. That explained the dark brown eyes which exactly matched the coloration of the Siberian Mountain butterfly whose range lay between the Khatanga and Olenek rivers. It can also be found in the Canadian Victoria Islands. Apparently the Home Office system for processing asylum seekers is like the Railtrack system for providing safe tracks – ignore it, throw a lot of money at it, and then run out of steam. Getting through the bureaucracy can take years and she'd quite faded from the view of the authorities by adapting to life in the station. I think Osaki at the beigel stand told me that her mother had been called Victoria. There were some retail staff who said she was a prostitute and that the Saturday man in Accessorize was her pimp. He turned out to be from Wolverhampton. A most charming man. I made the mistake of asking him about her during his lunch break, but he said that he wouldn't gossip about Natalia behind her back. Natalia? I knew her as Tati.

She gazed at me over her caffè latte, licked the froth from the delicate blond hairs fringing her upper lip and said that people called her by different names, that it didn't matter. I disagreed. You can't categorize something without an agreed-upon name.

'And where do you disappear to at night?' I asked, to delay her departure. She adjusted her ponytail in its Connex blue ruff, kissed me on both cheeks and then laid her forefinger against my lips.

'Shush,' she said.

Throughout my years at Victoria I have observed that extremes often walk side by side. The power-hungry are accompanied by lap-dogs. So it was with us. Unable to pin her down, Tati became indispensible to me. It seemed perfectly natural – our weekly dates, our shared affection for Victoria, the fact that she obviously liked older men – it had added up to only one thing in my mind: that we were in love. Marriage would inevitably follow and all her secrets would be mine. But for a lepidopterist I had committed a cardinal sin. I had allowed my feelings as an observer and collector to attach to the object of my observation: it was not me that she loved.

We were all invited to the reception – Connex employees, retail staff, the dinner-daddies, volunteers like myself. We took over the entire upstairs food hall area. She looked very beautiful in a glittering purple dress. As she left with her husband she threw me her bouquet of buddleia spikes and trailing nasturtiums. There was a small parcel of tissue paper taped to the ribbon securing the flowers. I unwrapped it with shaking fingers. She had given me a blue linen handkerchief, its colour a perfect Connex match. I waved it at her and the Saturday man from Accessorize as they gazed into each other's eyes and moved slowly towards the exit.

My Tati shimmered like a Purple Emperor the first and only time I ever saw her leave Victoria.

ERICA WAGNER

Miss Brooks

I HADN'T BEEN waiting long, only a few minutes, when Pat walked in.

'Sarah!' She saw me from where she stood at the door, taking off the Max Mara coat she'd bought one morning as we strolled uptown together ('Not just *un peu jeune*?' she'd gleamed at the assistant standing behind us as she smiled into the mirror). 'Darling!' she leaned over, kissed me on both cheeks, plopped down in the chair. 'Didn't keep you waiting? I just couldn't get off the phone. Honestly, children! You think the whole point of their growing up is to get out from under your feet – and of course, when they're teenagers, you never hear the end of it. *Why don't you leave me alone? Why can't I live by myself?* Then they turn thirty and bang, suddenly it's all your problem again.'

The waitress approached with menus; Pat waved them away. 'Two burgers,' she said, just slightly too loudly, as if the woman might not speak English, 'both rare, no buns, and one of those nice Greek salads. No dressing. Iced tea,' she pointed at me, 'and iced coffee.' She pointed at herself. 'Right?' she grinned at me, that familiar, irresistible beam. Never mind that right before she came I'd had a sudden craving for a chicken-salad sandwich; well, too late now.

'Is it Hannah?' I asked, when the waitress was gone. 'What's the story now?'

'Oh, they're off to court, would you believe.' Pat rolled her eyes. 'Settle! I said. For heaven's sake, settle! I told her I'd managed to settle with her father; she should be able to settle with Todd. Of course she looked at me like I was out of my mind. Or like I was a crone from Neanderthal times!' She laughed. Her face was almost unlined – or maybe we always look the same to our old friends, I don't know. Pat was Pat. 'You can imagine the response. Oh Mom, things are different now than they were in your day, the times they are a-changin' –' The waitress deposited our drinks, and Pat dribbled milk into her coffee; I squeezed a lemon slice into my tea. 'So,' she said. 'That's my excuse.' And she patted my hand.

'Tough for Hannah,' I said. I gave her a look I meant to say, I'm a woman of the world. I was so used to sitting here with Pat talking about lawyers and settlements – she often referred to her husbands simply by number, as in 'I can't remember if it was One that was allergic to shellfish, or Three' – I never expected I'd want to talk about those things myself. My eye drifted out the window of Burger Heaven, across the avenue. We were sitting right at the front, near the window. There are two levels of shops along a lot of Lex – where the old doll hospital is? That was one of them. All those nail places, too. Anyway, my gaze just drifted out, up to one of those second-floor places, and snagged on one of the signs – a psychic's. A neon eye and a crystal ball, a deck of cards. I'd probably seen it for years and never noticed. Then of course, it's amazing what you never notice. I never noticed when Al got himself a mobile phone. 'Al left a message on my machine the other day,' I said.

'Schmuck,' Pat said. 'That's the word. I wish I'd used it twenty years ago. His *secretary*? For Christ's sake. I always said Al never had any imagination.' Had she always said that? I can't say I was exactly sure. 'It's all right? The money? What you agreed?' I nodded, pulling my burger apart with a fork. It was fine, what we agreed, but things had changed. I did not consider that there would ever be tenants living in most of my house – cooking on my stove, sleeping in my bedroom – when I was living downstairs in the of course very pleasant flat where our maid used to live. Maria comes in once a week now, but you couldn't say it was the same thing. Pat says I should be grateful that I got the house at all.

A person gets used to certain things, that's all. When things change, well – you have to get used to something else. I like to remember my mother, who always said that a resourceful person could find enjoyment in almost anything – a bus ride, a piece of bread toasted to perfection, a sea shell on the beach.

'You've got to move on,' Pat said. 'I've said it before, I'll say it again. You know,' she said, squinting at me as if to see me better, 'I should introduce you to Dr Mankiewicz. He's a wonder-worker, you know.' She winked at me. I looked at her unlined face more closely. 'It never hurts to feel your best at a time like this. That's exactly what I said to Hannah, too – go to a spa! Take care of yourself! Slaving away at that publishing house – which has all been re-structured, did I tell you? Just to add to her woes. "Everyone's got a new title, Mom, and I don't know what any of them mean." As if I would! She's an executive vice-president, now – that's sounds terrific, I said; she's not so sure.' Pat took a last bite of her burger. She'd eaten half. In the old days she would have stubbed her cigarette out in the rest of the meat. She looked at me across the table. 'Listen to me,' she said. Neither of us spoke for a minute. 'It'll be fine,' she said. 'Fine.' She patted my hand again.

We left Burger Heaven together, stood in the thinning light of early afternoon and kissed each other on the cheek. She got into a cab, I started walking back to 78th Street. I didn't think too much about our conversation, except to notice, as I occasionally did, the way it rolled over me, like big waves; I sometimes had that feeling you get in the ocean when things just aren't in your control any more. But that neon sign, the psychic's sign, lodged in my mind – it must have, because a few weeks later I was downtown, in the Village, where I hardly ever go except there's the most wonderful little man down there, Ernesto he's called, and he mends my shoes. *Good to see you, Mrs Wainwright*, he'll always say when I come in; and though I bring my shoes to be fixed wrapped in a Gristede's bag, he always gives them back in a box, a new shoebox, plain and brown.

This time the storefront I noticed – just off Sixth Avenue – had a curtain of dark green moiré behind the neon. Madame Rosa, it said. Psychic. The neon was looped into cursive and looked enticing, somehow, like a finger crooked at you, drawing you in. The curtain curved back behind a shelf, on which was displayed a vase of pink roses, a little past their best, with a crystal ball, smaller than the kind of ball you'd use for lawn bowls, on one side, and a deck of cards on the other. Not an ordinary deck of cards. I bent down to look at them; they were long and thin and had different figures than you see when you're playing bridge. Tarot cards? I had never seen a deck of those before.

By the door, there was a sign. A plastic sign, like those ones they have outside doctors' offices, only this was bigger.

What is your Fate? Who should you Love?
Let Madame Rosa show you the Answers.
She speaks with the Cards, she speaks with the Crystal.

She can look into your Heart through
the lines on your Palm.
Find Peace. Find Happiness.
Madame Rosa can Help!
Prices start: $25.

I didn't go in, no. I hailed a taxi and went back uptown. But the next week, when my shoes were ready, I rang the bell. It was one of those little speaker phone things; I couldn't hear anything ring, so I pressed it twice.

'Yes?' A thin voice, like something on an old record, and impatient.

'I'm sorry,' I said, and I was – I suppose the bell was working properly after all and I had sounded preemptory, demanding. 'I didn't realize – I'd like to see Madame Rosa.' Those words came out of my mouth? Why yes, they did.

'Palm, crystal, cards?'

I hadn't thought about that. 'Palm,' I found myself saying, because that seemed simplest. Anyway, the crystal ball, those cards – they seemed, well, foreign. Don't get me wrong: I've seen the Pyramids, I've been to the Uffizi, I love *that* kind of foreign. Strange, I mean. Nothing to do with me.

Inside: a dingy front room. Beige carpet, stained. A very slight smell of damp – I'd gone down four steps, so the room was below the level of the street. The window was high up in the room, and the curtain let in a little light – the green of it made the room seem like a fishtank. A battered sofa. Two chairs, gold, the kind of chair you find around the table at a charity ball. A card table covered in baize with objects wrapped in cloth, cheap silk it looked like, on its surface. By the doorway into the hallway a little, big-eyed boy wearing a T-shirt and nothing else. 'Shoo,' said Madame Rosa to the child, and he vanished silently.

Madame Rosa was about my age, I suppose. Dark hair, dyed, and a gaze just as black. She was wearing a house-dress and slippers. She didn't look like a psychic. She looked like – I don't know. Like Maria. Like a maid.

I stood, holding my purse, the box with my shoes, not sitting on the sofa. Madame Rosa looked me up and down. 'Palm reading,' she said. 'Fifty dollars.'

'It says, "from twenty-five dollars" on your sign.'

She shrugged. 'You want twenty-five dollar reading? Okay. You get twenty-five dollar reading.' She pointed to one of the gold chairs. 'Sit.'

I did. She sat opposite me, lowering herself into her seat like there was a heavy weight on her shoulders. 'Take off your rings. Hands on the table.'

I removed my engagement ring, a single-carat, cushion-cut flawless diamond with a half-carat emerald on either side of the stone; Al's mother's ring. My wedding band, gold, with my initials and Al's inside. From my right hand a delicate ring in the Victorian style, set with sapphires; that had been my mother's. I took off my mother's ring every night; I didn't always wear it. But I couldn't remember the last time I'd taken off my wedding and engagement rings. I set them on the baize, close to my elbow, and put my hands flat on the table.

'Palms up,' said Madame Rosa, in a voice that indicated she'd met brighter sparks than me. I almost stood up to go – what kind of tone was that to take with me? Who did she think she was? What was I doing here, anyway? In this – *place*. Well. I didn't stand up. I would find out what I was doing here. That's how things were now.

Her hands were rough and dry. The backs of my hands rested in her palms. The room was dim, but she'd turned on a gooseneck lamp that stood near the table; my hands were in its circle of light. Her mouth was a little open. I could see her teeth. She looked up at me – right into my eyes, what my Aunt Caroline would have called a bold look; Aunt Caroline didn't much approve of boldness. Bold was only a step away from sassy, and to tell you the truth this look Madame Rosa gave me was nearer sassy than bold. But I held steady: I looked right back, like I'd never looked back at Aunt Caroline. Madame Rosa took her eyes off mine, glanced back down at my hands, and sat back, folding her own hands on the table in front of her.

'Sad,' she said. 'Not always, but now.' Her voice had a darkness to it, like the room; her accent wasn't like Maria's, I thought. Maria was from Columbia. Wherever Madame Rosa was from, it wasn't Columbia. I'd kept my hands on the table when she let them go, still like landed fish – now she reached over, stabbed with her finger what seemed to me an indeterminate place in my right hand. 'Money troubles, too.' She gave her little shrug again. 'The future,' she said. 'You can change it. Not true of everyone. Not everyone can change.' She said the last like she was making a concession; like it was something she'd rather not admit.

Now, I'll tell you the truth. When I heard what she said – sadness, money troubles – you know, I felt a shiver down my spine. When I was a girl, if you shivered for no reason, we'd say *someone's just walked over your grave* – it felt like that. I didn't move. I sat there with my hands on the table. She looked at me, flat in the eye.

'Twenty-five dollars,' she said.

That woke me up. 'That's it?'

She shrugged and got up, ran her rough square hands down the front of her house-dress.

I almost didn't remember to put my rings on; but when I looked down for my purse, there they were, on the table.

Harder to get them over my knuckles these days, just enough that I notice. Madame Rosa and I weren't getting any younger: no wonder she was in a hurry.

I didn't have any five-dollar bills in my purse; and I wondered if I was meant to tip her. There are things you tip for in this city where it doesn't matter – doesn't matter a damn, my father would say and make me blush – whether you like the service or not: you tip. Tipping averts disaster. Cabs, restaurants, doormen. Those are the rules. Better safe than sorry, I thought. I gave her a ten and a twenty. She didn't say thank you. She nodded, and slipped the bills into the pocket of her dress. I could hear a noise from the back, a crash, like something falling off a shelf. Her eyes darted back; I remembered the little boy. 'I'll let myself out,' I said.

On the street, the bright sun made me squint after that green, submerged light. I'd remembered my shoes. I ought to have taken the subway home: but there was a cab, right there. I hailed it and got in.

Those ads in *The New Yorker* cost more than you'd think. Not the big ads; just the little ones, down the side of the page. Pat reads *The New Yorker*; I never did. It made me feel dumb. I liked something a bit, well, lighter; what's a magazine for if not to entertain you? Though of course, I always liked the cartoons. Someone gave us a big book of them when I was young, and I used to look at them and laugh, even at the ones I didn't understand, the ones about the Depression and Prohibition.

I saw a girl in Burger Heaven reading *The New Yorker*, that's when I thought of it. A pretty girl, with very short, very dark hair and those fashionable half-frame glasses, where the half of the frame goes over the top. She was leaning her head on her hand and looking hard at the magazine, turning the pages slowly, sipping an iced coffee. The kind of girl I never imagined I'd ever be when I was young – a smart girl – and yet, there was something about her that made me realize: she thinks something's missing, too. She wants something, even if she doesn't know what it is. It isn't all there, in that magazine. But that's where she goes to look.

Now, it hadn't taken very long to realise that what Madame Rosa was purveying was not insight but hokum. That night, after my taxi ride uptown, my repaired Ballys neatly back in my closet, I laughed out loud in my own kitchen. Why, anyone could have guessed I was sad – anyone could have guessed I might have had some money troubles – what on earth would a woman like me be doing in Madame Rosa's if – well, if some tumult hadn't occurred? But I'd been fooled. The crystal ball, the darkened room, my hands, naked, flat on the table: I was willing. Silly girl. I always was a silly girl, everyone said. Only now, I wasn't girl, of course. Too bad.

It was later that same night I had a different kind of thought. That the shiver I'd felt was real. That there was no fooling about that. And maybe – but that was just plain ridiculous. But it kept me up all night, that ridiculous thought. I had an image. I started to have a plan. So eventually I called *The New Yorker* and enquired after their rates.

Miss Brooks
Psychic consultation
(212) 555–1676

It was a while before my little ad – in a cursive typeface, *Shelley Script Allegro* they call it, in hot pink which I thought would look striking, like a kind of neon on the page – actually appeared. I took my time. I did my research. When was I last in the stacks of the Society Library? But there I sat, for hours, on a stool, like a girl doing her homework – which is exactly what I was. *Tasseomancy*: divination by the pattern of leaves in a teacup. *Abacomancy*: the act of foretelling the future by the patterns made in dust; sometimes the ashes of the recently deceased may be used. *Tyromancy*: divination by the patterns made in the coagulation of cheese.

'You're – what?' Pat said. We were in Burger Heaven again. Our lunch had just arrived. I told her. Well, I had to, didn't I? She'd find out. I'd ordered a brass plaque to go next to the front door, very discreet, very Fifth-Avenue-Upper-Eighties-Doctor. I had the copy of *The New Yorker*, with the ad; it was on the table between us.

'Brooks. My maiden name. I thought that was a good idea,' I said.

'Well,' Pat said. She was blinking behind her yellow-tinted glasses. 'I suppose it is.' Had I ever seen Pat at a loss for words? I tried not to smile. 'But how –'

'I've been studying,' I said, truthfully. 'And I think I have' – this was harder to get out, but it's funny how when you say things they seem true – 'I think I have a gift.' Pat blinked again. Then she seemed to get her old self back, and laughed, loud enough for other diners to turn and stare.

'You're a hoot,' she said. 'A real hoot. All right,' she said, 'I'll tell you what.' She took a decisive forkful of burger, chewed and swallowed. 'I'll be your first customer. How's that? I won't even expect a discount. What are you charging?'

Now, this isn't what I'd expected. It's not what I'd

121

expected at all. So much for my psychic powers, you might say! Well, it's not meant to work like that. I never said I was a seer. Still, I looked Pat in the eye. 'A hundred dollars,' I said. 'For the initial consultation. Forty-five minutes.'

Pat raised a pencilled brow. 'Fine,' she said, flatly. 'Sign me up.'

I felt terrible after we parted. The feeling in the pit of my stomach I used to get before a dance. But my legs took me to Smythson, on Madison, where I spent an unconscionable amount of money on a wide brown leather book with pale blue paper that was embossed with gold on its cover: Appointments. I put it by the telephone. And do you know – the phone began to ring. But I'd promised Pat the first appointment; my several callers were all fitted in after the date we'd fixed. It amazed me how amenable they were to the times I suggested. 'That's fine,' they said. 'Whatever you think is best,' said one woman, who I guessed was young, but of course it's always hard to tell on the phone. I discovered I was looking forward to matching my impressions of their voices with their faces, their selves. Five appointments. Five.

Now, I had no plans to do any divining by watching mould grow on cheese. Miss Brooks, as I said, was who I was before I was married: Miss Brooks was me. I was a simple person, I thought; best to keep things simple. And while I read about the lines of the head and the lines of the heart, the mount of Mars and the mount of Venus, the hand you are given, the hand that you make – while I read about all that I found myself recalling conversations I thought I'd long forgotten; those rare conversations where you feel you really get to the heart of things. *I never knew you felt that way. Well, yes, only I never thought* – looking out at the flat water of Gardiner's Bay, walking through Central Park.

Some of them were even with Al; and I didn't mind that nearly as much as I thought I would.

Pat was prompt. Five minutes early, in fact, which was rather interesting in itself; Pat was not always what you would call a punctual person. It was a hot August day; she was wearing a bright shift dress and pumps; her big dark Jackie-O glasses covered her eyes and her hair, I could tell, had just been frosted. Someone seeing us, when I opened the door, might have thought we looked alike, even though I was dark and she was fair and our clothes were by no means the same – I had on wide linen trousers, a nice blue silk blouse and my patent-leather Dr Scholl's – but that person might have thought, I know that kind of woman. But Pat was surprised, I could tell – maybe she thought I'd be wearing a kaftan, or have one of those Indian beads pasted to my forehead.

'Hello,' I said. 'Come in.'

She touched the wooden edge of my shining new plaque before she entered; 'Very nice,' she said, instead of Hello.

She peered around my house as if she'd never seen it before. Nothing was different, except for the card table set up before the fireplace; I'd covered it with a lovely cream silk Jacquard cloth I had; it fell right to the floor, because really it was too big for the small table, but I liked the effect. I'd put a vase of yellow roses in the fire grate. 'A cup of tea?' I asked her.

'All right,' she said, and then recovered herself, blushed a little even, I think. 'Yes please.' And then she smiled. 'Yes please, Miss Brooks.' She looked at me as if we were in a conspiracy; as if she was trying to see behind my face, that's the only way I can put it. I smiled at her, very pleasantly, and went to make the tea, which I served in my best china.

'Have a seat,' I said, when I handed her the cup, and indicated the little chair I'd set out by the card table, the one nearest the front door. I took the other, opposite. I had no tea.

'No crystal ball?' Pat said. She'd pushed her glasses up on top of her head. I noticed her mouth was a little tight, like she was trying to seem more amused than she was. It's amazing what you see if you really look at people, you know.

'I'll look at your hands,' I said. I'd decided that *read your palm* wasn't the expression I wanted to use; I wasn't going to make myself a sideshow. 'Put them on the table. Take off your rings.'

She did just as I told her. She struggled to get one of them off, an opal set in platinum she'd bought for herself in Singapore, years ago. I sat quietly until there was a little pile of jewellery by her wrist. She'd put her palms on the table so I could see the backs of her hands; the way the veins had raised themselves from the flesh, the way the skin had fallen away from the knuckles, the brown spots that persisted despite the assiduous use of vanishing cream. The new manicure: coral, for summer. 'Turn your hands over,' I said.

Palms up, now. She looked into my eyes. Her own eyes were pale blue, ringed with dark mascara clumped a little precariously on her lashes. 'I may not speak of the past,' I said in a quiet voice. This is what I planned to say; I'd written it, I liked the words in my mouth. 'I may not speak of the future. I may not even speak of the present: but I make you a promise: I will speak only the truth.' I touched my fingertips to hers, and I felt it, the change in her – it thrilled me, I knew what it was, though I hardly knew how I did. Something stripped away. She was afraid: it was there in my fingers, her fear. I didn't mean to make her afraid. I covered her palms with my own; hers were cold and mine were warm.

'It's all right,' I said. *Miss Brooks* said. 'Let's begin.'

CAREY JANE HARDY

Face to Face

I CLIMB THE eleven polished steps twice a month and talk
to Wil. Our conversation is enlightening for both of us, I
think. We talk of things that are not always understood
outside our four walls. And these moments nurture me and
show me that my memory – intact and clear though
strangely severed from its context – allows the picture of
tomorrow to grow a little clearer. That is important to me.
Yesterday is passed. Tomorrow is still to be lived, albeit
differently.

Knowing this, I wonder why it took me so long to tell him
about the poster. I was remembering the Isles of Scilly and
suddenly I began to tell him. 'Wil,' I asked. 'Would you
know what to do if you met a polar bear?'

'No.' Wil is always direct.

'I saw a poster once which told me. It was in the most
unlikely place, but there it was, waiting for me to see it.'

It was a blue poster, and white of course. Blue and white.
Although my memory cannot conjure up the exact words of
its advice, I was left with a firm impression that you can
never outrun a polar bear. There is little point in trying.
Better to stand still and face it. And if you shoot, then shoot
to kill.

The strangest thing of all, of course, is that there are no
polar bears on the Isles of Scilly, come winter or summer,

come rain or shine, come storms upon the sea or mist from the mainland. No polar bears. So did I dream that? Could I really have seen such a poster? Yes. I did. I remember.

I have more occasion to remember it now. I remember things that I have seen in my past life. And so I talk about them with Wil. He finds them fascinating. Sometimes I hear the sound of his pen against the paper as he records something that I have said. When I hear that sound I give myself a mental pat on the back. It is as though I've scored a point, given him what he wanted, something he can use. He likes to write about me. My story grows like a plant in this greenhouse of fragmented memories.

When I told him about the poster, he asked me, quite casually, whether I'd ever seen a polar bear. I think it was a throwaway question, not meant for the record. Just polite small talk, I suppose: a chat between the courses, a cleansing of the palate before the meat of our deeper conversations. Yet I surprised him. Because I hesitated.

Wil is fascinated by hesitations. I know that, because occasionally I can hear the leather of his chair squeak as he leans towards me, waiting for me to speak again. Once I thought I could hear his heart beat moments before my own.

'You have, haven't you?' he said.

And so I told him.

'Sometimes,' I said, 'I dream of the polar bear. It always stands so still, watching me, as though it knew I would be there, that tonight I would dream.'

'Do you know that you are dreaming?' asked Wil.

Surely I must know. Even in my subconscious I must know that I have never really stood upon that frozen lid of the world, staring across the ice at this beautiful and majestic creature. Yet at the same time, as I stand there, in my dreamer's safety, I am totally exposed by an all-consuming ignorance of the fact that this is a dream. I feel only the awful fear of present reality. The polar bear, the most dangerous predator of the Arctic, looks at me and I look back, and nothing stands between me and my fate except the fear I must first experience.

'No,' I said at last. 'I don't know that I am dreaming.'

'And this dream is recurring?'

'Yes.'

'And it started after you saw the poster?'

It is not like Wil to pre-empt my answers.

'No,' I said. 'No, it started long before that.'

It would be a quick death, I sometimes think. One swipe of its paw would be enough to break my neck. Quick and kind. Yet there is no such thing as a kind polar bear, or a gentle predator. This creature cannot know that I would not harm it, that we could stand here like this for always, and I would not, even in my fear, tire of looking at its splendour. Still it stares at me with its black eyes, frozen in time. And every time I wake, I do so with the knowledge that still the attack has not come. Still I am safe with my fear.

'What are you afraid of?' asked Wil.

'Darkness,' I said.

'Yes,' said Wil. 'Of course.' His voice was not patronizing. He has a rare gift of never expressing either patronage nor pity. This is a constant source of comfort to me: that in this present darkness he does not diminish me.

'Tell me,' he had said on my very first visit to him. 'When did you first realize that you were going blind?'

It had come gradually. The realization, I mean: not the blindness. That had come all too quickly, with so little warning that over the few weeks before the final curtain fell, I had groped for any form of denial. And even then, I believed that the light would return.

Over the years I had suffered with periodic insomnia, and long ago I learned, after many fruitless struggles, that the best way of passing the time was to lie quietly, to empty my mind of everything except the belief that, eventually, morning would come. The gentle unfolding of the dawn heralded the fact that the ordeal was nearly over, and that I had coped with wakefulness.

So in my early blindness I waited for the light. Yet time ticked on. The dawn never came. There was only darkness. And finally I knew that I was blind.

When I had told Wil this, on that first visit, he had been quiet for a long time. I wondered if he was trying to envisage himself in that place. Then he asked me, 'Do you see anything at all now?'

'Shadows, sometimes,' I said. 'Fragments of shadows. But nothing real.'

'Can you see my shadow?' said Wil. 'If I pass my hand in front of your eyes, do you see anything?'

I waited, wondering if he was moving his hand as he spoke, an experiment in his own existence. 'No,' I said. 'The shadows are not real. They belong no where.'

'Thank you,' he said. And I heard the scratch of his pen upon the paper.

The polar bear lives in twilight for half of the year. For six months the sun does not rise above the horizon. During that time the bear must use its remarkable sense of smell to track its food. 'Perhaps I should try that,' I said to Wil. He laughed.

'How do you track?' he asked. 'How do you find your way?'

'By sounds. I visualize by the clues I hear. Like this room. The wooden steps, the leather chair, the pencil. There's a postbox down there in the street.'

'How d'you know that?'

'I've heard them empty it. The engine of the van stops. Then comes the jangling of the keys, the dull thud of letters into the bag. Then the keys again. The slam of the post van door. The engine starts up. There's a collection at about quarter past two. I hear your digital watch. Then the van arrives. Sometimes it's late. Nearer twenty or twenty-five past.'

'I'm impressed,' said Wil.

'It comes of necessity,' I told him. 'I have to colour my surroundings.'

'Colour?' said Wil. 'That's an interesting word to use.'

'I used to be able to see,' I explain. 'Now I see in shadows, but I remember in colours.'

'Do you dream in colour?'

'There's no need,' I told him. 'The polar bear is always white.'

Some nights I look for the colours. The fur is white, the eyes are black. The snow is white, the sea is black.

'But the sun?' said Wil. 'Is the sun not gold? Is the sky not blue?'

I laughed. 'When you're facing a polar bear, do you have time to look at the sky?'

In my dream I must have some recall of this conversation, because sometimes I do try to take my eyes from the eyes of the polar bear and look up at the sky. I cannot do it. Yet there are times when the polar bear is not too close. It is further away, across a stretch of dark water, balancing on a raft of ice. Behind it is the sky, sometimes dark and sometimes bright, an endless panorama of shade and light. It has no colour at all. When the bear is closer – beautiful and white – I do not see the sky. Yet I realize of late, that I can hear the claws against the snow: black claws on white snow, scratching against my dream.

It is nearly four years since I lost my sight. Another strange choice of word. *Lost*. As though I went out one day and mislaid something, or forgot where I had put it. When I hear that people have 'lost a limb' or 'lost a loved one', a picture stays in my mind of legs and loved ones floating forlornly in some vast lost-property depot, waiting to be reclaimed. Yet I have no picture of what my sight would look like in that context, existing alone, fragmented from me. For that word – lost – suggests that it is only my knowledge of this capacity that is missing, that it must exist elsewhere, waiting to be reclaimed if only I could remember how.

Such a possibility is hopeless, however. They have told me so. Cells have died and cannot regenerate. Nerves have been damaged and cannot be restored. I cannot ever learn to see again. This loss is permanent.

Four years on, there is strange comfort in this. I do not have to live day by day with possibilities, clutching at the maybe. There is a certainty in my lack. This is who I am now.

'And who is that?' Wil asked me.

'The me who does not see,' I told him.

'And is that different from the you who could see? What I mean is,' he said, leaning forward in his chair, 'are you fundamentally different in any other respect – apart from the physical blindness – from the person you were when you could see?'

'Should I be?'

'Forget the supposition at this point,' said Wil. 'For now, simply deal with the initial question. Are you different?'

This question has lasted us some time: months it must be. I have thought about it often. At first I always came back to the same problem. How do I know whether or not I am different until I know what or who I really am. Who is the real me?

'Do you believe in the real you?' said Wil.

And I told him that I did, with an assurance that surprised me. For I had not been aware of such a faith.

Even before I went blind I could not see myself as others saw me, or indeed, as I saw others. I could look at my hands, my feet, but I could not see my face except as a mirror image, or as a celluloid printout, or a vague reflection in a shop window. I could not stand back and see the whole being, in proportion. The reflection in the mirror, the face in the photograph came as a shock, producing a feeling of disbelief that such things represented me. For this was not how I saw myself. This was not the imprint I carried in my mind's eye. I carried, instead, an unchanging sense of myself through the years, that possibly had little to do with the reality, yet was more than real.

Now I do not even have the mirror, or the photographs. I can only remember what I think I looked like four years ago. And as this gap of time extends to ten years – fourteen – forty – so the gap between the memory picture and the reality will become even more extreme. I will have to imagine the slow process of change, how the lines will deepen around my sightless eyes, how my hair will gradually lose its colour and my jaw slacken. I will not see what others see, and I cannot ask them. Even if I did ask them, there is no way I could test the truth or the insight of their reply.

The only person who would tell me, I believe, is Wil. And I could not ask him, for despite our meetings, despite the depth of his knowledge of me now, there is a certain impartiality in his view of me that I doubt we could broach.

'Has it struck you,' I say to Wil, 'that now there is only one face I ever see?'

'And you see that only in a dream.'

'Yes.'

'Do you not dream of other faces?'

'Not that I remember.'

This is true. For in my other dreams I am blind. I dream as the blind dream, by touch and sound and smell and sensation. I cannot dream of faces I have never seen.

And this thought brings me to the realization that I have no idea what Wil looks like. My knowledge of him began after my blindness. What I know of him is his voice, the characteristic intakes of breath that denote a certain emotion, the sound of his limbs moving in the confinement of a leather chair, the scent of his clothes, the resonance of his laughter, the silent pause of his understanding. This is the Wil I believe I know.

The only other sense of sight at my disposal is that of touch. When we were first introduced we shook hands. His was large and firm, the palm broad, the fingers short and square. I have remembered that and it has become part of my picture of him.

A blind person – a person like myself – cannot study a human face from the safe distance of impartiality. Only by touch could I see him. Only by touching his face with my fingers, could I fill in those other mysterious details about Wil. And even after four years there is an understandable social shyness about such things. People like Wil and myself do not – perhaps cannot – speak so blatantly with our hands.

Besides, I tell myself, this would still not show me Wil. It would be an instant in time, coloured too boldly by reticence on his part and shyness on mine, and I would read these things in his face for every second my fingers lingered there. To know a face in all its moods it must be studied quietly and frequently from beyond the awareness of the other being: as Wil, perhaps, must study mine.

I can study but one face now. It comes to me like a ghostly visitation out in some vast plain beyond my memory. I can study frequently – though perhaps never impartially – and gaze again and again as though it were for the first time and the last. There exists here a fearful familiarity as I look once more upon the only face I've seen in four years, that of the polar bear.

'How would you feel if the dreams were to stop?'

The question startled me.

'Stop dreaming?'

'Yes.'

And suddenly I am rendered newly blind: a blind person without a face, without knowledge of faces, with only memory.

'I don't know,' I said.

'Do you think they will stop?'

'There must be an outcome,' I said. 'One of two possible outcomes. Either the bear will attack, or it will find some other prey.'

'And leave you?'

'Yes.'

'And who are you? Who is this person who sees the polar bear.'

'Me.'

'And you are not blind?'

'No.'

'Why should that be?'

'I suppose,' I said, 'because it came before I was blind.'

'The dream?'

'The polar bear.'

'And when it first began, this dream, did you know by then that one day you would be blind?'

I felt, as I had always felt, the heavy pain of knowledge. 'Yes,' I told him. 'It was a degenerative condition. I knew for years that it might happen.'

'And it did.'

'Yes.'

'But this condition only affected your eyes. It can do no further damage.' Wil did not phrase this as a question. He was simply repeating a fact he knew. One of the many facts he knew about me.

'That's right,' I said. 'This is as bad as it gets.'

'What are you most afraid of?' asked Wil. 'Of the dream itself, or the absence of the dream?'

'I'm not afraid *of* the dream,' I said. 'I'm afraid *in* the dream. I'm afraid of the bear.'

'Still?'

'What?'

'Still afraid, after all these years, of something that has never once tried to harm you?'

I sat quite still, remembering: the white fur, the black eyes, the pointed muzzle, the long forelegs, the high shoulders, the claws scratching in the snow, the eerie stillness of the arctic winter. It wouldn't be like that of course, not all the time. An icy wind would blow.

'It will attack one day,' I said.

'How do you know?'

Because of the fear, the fear that comes with the inevitability of it all, amidst the waiting.

'It must,' I said. 'It makes sense. It knows I'm there. It's seen me.'

I heard the leather creak. Cotton rubbed against cotton as he uncrossed his legs. He took a short sharp breath through his nostrils. 'What would you say to the notion,' said Wil, 'that the polar bear can't see you? That the polar bear is blind?'

I heard my own breath, shorter and deeper than his. Then I began to laugh. 'Don't be ridiculous, Wil!'

Again, the short, sharp sniff. 'What is so ridiculous about it?'

'A blind polar bear? It wouldn't survive. It would be dead within weeks. I've known this bear for years.'

'You take this relationship very literally, don't you? Just you and the bear, standing there in the snow for years and years?'

'Believe me,' I said. 'It can see me. A blind bear is a dead bear.'

'Which makes it far weaker than you,' said Wil. 'For you are blind and still very much alive.'

'But remember,' I said, 'in the dream, I'm not blind yet.'

'Quite,' said Wil.

It is months before the dream comes again. I become impatient. For I feel that some outcome is approaching. The absence of the bear only prolongs the end. The seasons have changed since that particular dialogue with Wil. We have talked of other things. It is as though something is on hold, and it unnerves me a little.

Finally I dream. It is April. I dream against the sound of

the rain. The sound is of rushing water in my ears, as though the ice is beginning to break up, as though the thaw approaches. It is some moments before I see the bear. It is further away than it has ever been before, and I am aware of a sense of disappointment, as though I had expected it to be much, much closer. It lifts its head and now I am more sure than ever that it has seen me. We stand, our eyes fixed on each other. I see the black tongue flick out and over the black nose. Even at this distance I can see the droplets of water shining on its face.

Then it moves. Slowly, very slowly it begins to move towards me. The giant paws stalk the snow and with every stride the black claws make their rhythmic contact, scratching, tapping against the freeze. I watch, fascinated rather than fearful, sensing only the anticipation of a long-awaited meeting. Until, that is, I see that the bear is no longer walking.

She covers the distance between us with bounding leaps, with ever increasing speed and power. Closer and closer now, white against white, until I look into the eyes, wild in their flight, and see fire within ice. It will be momentary. Soon it will be over, a fraction of a second longer and then . . .

And then she plunges joyfully into the flowing water where the ice has melted the space between us. In slow motion I watch as the spray – blue and white and gold against the arctic sun – rises in a triumphant arch around her. In the seconds before its brilliance blinds me I see in a flash of time all the splendour of this strange domain, in every colour, hue and tone, as loud as the clashing of cymbals against my mind.

I awake, crying out even in my release, knowing that in

this moment of supreme beauty there is a loss for which I can never atone.

I walk in the soft April rain and lift my face to feel the elements against my skin. There will be droplets in my hair, bright perhaps against my lashes, like tears. I climb the eleven wooden steps to Wil's room and feel the brass plaque beneath my hands. I knock and after a moment I hear the door open. I step inside and find my way, my old familiar way, to the chair beside his own.

'She's gone,' I tell him.

'She?'

'The polar bear.'

'I didn't know it was a she.'

'Didn't you?'

I hear him smile.

'I think,' I say, 'that with her I was more supremely myself than at any other time.'

'The real you?'

'Hers was the last face, the last glance, the last vast whiteness before the darkness. That's why I held on so long. And do you know something, Wil? At the end it wasn't even dark.'

The leather creaks. 'What happened at the end?'

'At the end,' I say, 'I don't think she even saw me.' And I tell him what happened. And how I had been blinded by the light.

In telling him, in making this strange confession, I sense that my time with Wil is nearly over. There has been growth and change. I am different – or if not different, then I have moved on. These meetings, twice a month, every month, month after month, have served a purpose. Perhaps it is time to move on further and let go again. With this thought there comes an inevitable sadness, a recognition of loss. And I am not sure if I am ready to lose this too.

My mind floods with memories, both silly and sweet, and there is a pride in the very sweetness of what has been achieved. I will not forget that. Perhaps I will tell him one day. For now I think, a new era has begun – a different me, within my own reality. Perhaps now, I will dream as other people do, in shadows of colour. But there is something I still need to do. One final step to take.

I stand up.

'Wil?' I say.

'Yes?'

'Can I see your face?'

It is a moment before I hear him stand too. He takes my hands and lifts them to his face. Only now do I press my thumbs flat against his eyebrows, and my fingers around the shape of his jaw, and the palms of my hands across his hair. And so at last I see him.

I am glad I waited until now. Four years have given my fingers a sensitivity I did not have before. And strangely, I realize, I was wrong before in my estimation of its value. I see him with greater clarity than I could have imagined, face to face. And it is as though the sun had plumbed the depths of the ocean floor, and flooded with light a hitherto sunless sea.

VICTORIA BRIGGS

Shoe Fly Baby

'I MUST BE paying you too much money.'

Uncle Abdi sighs, wets his middle finger and counts the notes straight into Halim's palm, slapping each one down like a costly high-five.

Halim laughs. Today is payday and tomorrow is his day off.

'But the trainers are Nike, Uncle. The best.'

Uncle Abdi grunts and finishes counting. With his counting hand he reaches for his cigarettes and pushes one into the open space between his black moustache and dark speckled chin. Uncle Abdi's cigarettes are perfumed, Turkish, unfiltered. Halim smokes Marlboro Lights.

'Say hello to Elif for me. And tell your father he still owes me that card game!'

Uncle Abdi slaps Halim on the back. Halim smiles. He folds the twenty-pound notes in half and slides them down into the front pocket of his Levis. They shake hands goodbye. Halim leaves the shop and starts walking down the Lanes.

Green Lanes is a twenty-four hour traffic-chain, linking North London extremis to West End metropolis. It is a thoroughfare between one place and another, a dirty concrete hyphen linking downtown urban to leafy suburban. It

140

is supple and long-limbed, stretching north from Stoke Newington and up through the whole of Haringey. It is little Athens, little Istanbul, little Larnaca. A piece from each clusters its edges and sings soft-tongued of Mother Home. Above the singing, horns blare. Drivers weave and dodge, trade insults, trade blows, wave one finger from a wound-down window. The horns blare and the exhaust pipes empty their noxious cargo into the sky above. On the Lanes, even the pigeons get asthma.

Halim makes his way to the blue-fronted sports shop where Memduh works. The shop is close to Abdi's place and it takes Halim less than five minutes to get there. He pushes the door open. Inside the shop, rows of Nikes are stacked next to rows of Adidas, Reebok, Pumas, Converse and Vans. Halim can stand and look at trainers the way some people can stand and look at the stars. In his mind he runs through an old dream, the one where he's just won the lottery and he gets to buy as many pairs of trainers as he wants. From this shop alone he could take more than twenty. The music playing is deep house. Its bass notes throb against the soles of Halim's feet. He taps one foot to the rhythm. From across the shop floor Memduh spots him.

'Hey, bruv!'

Memduh walks towards Halim and extends a hand. Halim takes it into his own and the two hands lock briefly before sliding palms, squeezing fingers and banging fists in a well-practiced ritual of friendship.

'Good, good. You got my Nikes, man?'

'Yeah. And I gave you a staff discount. Put them through as my own.'

'Wicked, man. I owe you one.'

Halim and Memduh go way back. Since they both

skipped school together and played football in the park, wearing baggy Galatasaray tops and smoking stale dog-ends. For pocket money they hung around the gaming cafés in the evening, running errands for the men inside who played the card tables and sat drinking mint tea while keeping one eye on the card dealer and calling out 'twist'.

Uncle Abdi ran a gaming café once, in the days before he had his own grocery shop. He tells Halim there is no real money in the gambling business. Too many smart players and too many pay-outs to the protection squads who charged by the table and who didn't give credit.

'Second worst business to whoring,' says Uncle Abdi, 'stick to grocery, son.'

Whoring. There are two brothels in Haringey. One is a neon-fronted massage parlour near the tube station. The other is shuttered and discreet and sits on one of the side roads that form the Haringey Ladder. This is the 'Selective Modelling Agency', the one Halim prefers. Debra works here and Halim visits her almost every payday.

'You didn't come last week!' chides Debra. 'I thought you'd skipped the country.'

'Miss me, babe?' Halim laughs.

Debra turns to look at Halim full on. Her pale hair is splayed about her shoulders and she wears a red dress that fits as close as a hug.

'Miss these, lover?' she asks. Her voice is an octave deeper and she holds up a pair of black leather shoes with a pointed toe and a five-inch heel. The shoes are newly polished and Debra's hair is like a gold wing reflected in their black light.

Halim sets down the bag with the trainers in it and takes off his jacket. Debra's room is lamp-lit and homely.

142

Wooden floorboards with a rug laid over them at an angle gives the place a modern feel. The bed is wood-framed and lapped by a pink cotton duvet cover. Somewhere outside the room, soft music plays, and somewhere within the music – or in a room just behind it – there is the noise of a man gasping for life, air, joy.

Halim sits on the rug, cross-legged, with his back against the bed. He likes to sit this way so that he is nearer to Debra's feet. She looks down at him from her place near the wardrobe and thinks how young he looks that way. Not so much older than herself. She holds out the shoes before him,

'You want me to put these on?'

The madam of the Selective Modelling Agency is a six-foot bruiser named Ali. He earns a good living off the girls and is proud that they are the best in the borough. With a head for business, he knows that his continued profit margin rests with the house's reputation.

'No fags, no nonces, no perverts,' says Ali.

Ali runs a straightforward business and is not tempted to expand into other areas of the market that he hears about in the West End. Those stories about leather masks, or men on men, make his teeth tingle as if he just ate something cold.

'Just ain't right,' he says to his girls.

Debra works a six-day week and takes Sundays off to shop with her girlfriends from the Agency. They always go for a coffee first and then shop for a couple of hours before visiting the nail bar for a buff and polish. Ali likes his girls to look classy. This week Debra's nails are oxblood red. Tomorrow she'll choose the tiger stripes.

Debra looks at Halim cross-legged on the rug and thinks it makes a nice change to be the one in charge. Apart from the home life and the extra year or so, the two of them are not that different. Debra had been a latchkey kid before she was tall enough to reach the latch. Chilblains on her feet and hands, garnered from hours sat on the doorstep waiting for somebody to come home, still hurt in the cold. Halim is the only man who ever looked at her feet and told her they were beautiful. She lets herself believe him.

From his position on the floor, Halim sees the shoes dangle above him, held out like a dark tease or a dirty promise. Yes, he tells Debra. He would like her to put the shoes on.

Debra perches on the edge of the bed close to where Halim sits, watching. She puts the shoes down on the rug so that they stand side by side. Then she slips her feet out of her existing shoes and pours them languorously into this pair.

Halim is all wide eyes and shallow breaths. The room is warm and a bead of sweat cradles in the bow of his upper lip.

He sits and watches. The shoe is a hungry mouth. Debra slides the red-tipped toes of her right foot into the corresponding right shoe. The sole follows, with arch seeking leather and heel finding form above the five-inch spike. Then the left foot does the same. The shoes yawn wide-open and then they swallow her whole. In the quiet of the bedroom Halim thinks he almost hears them sigh.

Debra eases herself up from the bed with her arms held out a little to her side so that she can keep herself steady in the tricky getting-up part. The shoes are not comfortable. The weight of her body is thrown forward on to the balls of her feet and she has to take a moment to adjust to the new centre of balance within herself. She worries about twisting over on her ankle and spraining it, or worse. Ali would not be pleased

144

if she couldn't turn tricks for a month because she was laid up in bed with a plaster cast and crutches. She wouldn't be allowed to work. Ali would worry too much about getting a name for peddling cripple girls. He would worry a lot more if he knew what Halim's tastes were, that they were being catered for under his roof. Oh if Ali ever knew! He would flash his teeth, flash his fists; save his open palm for Debra. Girls with bruised faces are not good for business.

So Debra keeps it to herself and doesn't say a word, not even to the other girls. Halim is her secret, her perk of the job – a treat to herself for working so hard. He's her double choc-chip ice cream when she's supposed to be on a diet, her new lipstick and mascara when she's supposed to be paying back her debts.

Debra walks over the rug to the edges of the room where the floorboards lay exposed. She likes the sound that her heels make when they clack against the bare boards. Halim's face is a picture too. A hundred times she's wished she had a camera to capture it on film. A hundred times she's decided that the risk of her heels being heard outside the room was well worth the taking. Besides, she knows she can lie well when she has to.

In the thirty minutes they have together, Debra guides the shoes through a routine of maximum movement and display. She likes to dance for Halim. She hums along to the music playing outside the room and lets her body move from the feet up. She used to move more with her upper body but she quickly realised that Halim's gaze never strayed above the ankle. Now she concentrates her energy into her footwork. She Dorothy-clicks her heels for him, stands on tiptoe, uses the back of the armchair as a barre and moves through the remembered positions of past ballet lessons. She is amazed how good her plié still is.

In these shoes she feels tall enough to be a model, and in her mind she makes it so she is a model and this length of room is her catwalk. She moves from the hip and takes long rolling strides the way she's seen it done on TV. At the end of one length she pauses for the flash bulbs, lips parted, eyes focussed into the hazy middle distance. Then she spins herself round on one heel and begins the sashay back in the opposite direction. The crowd roars.

When she tires of dancing and treading the catwalk, Debra sits down in the armchair opposite Halim. She slips a foot outside of its shoe and begins to toy with it; a cat with a rat, her toes mauling leather.

Halim's eyes are as wide as they can be when she makes to crush the shoe like a discarded cigarette. Debra laughs – it's just her teasing toes. Look! She hands the shoe to Halim. It's as perfect as before. Only more so, now it sits here in his hands. He touches it to make it real, to hold in his hand what the eye had previously only held in its gaze. Her smell is caught inside the shoe. Halim breathes in deep.

The bedside clock shows Debra when the half hour is up. The last few minutes are always a little hard going – her toes get sore from the pinch of the leather and her hamstrings ache from their stretch to infinity.

Halim pushes his arms down the sleeves of his jacket and bundles up the plastic sports bag. He looks to Debra to bring his time with her to a close.

'Next week?' she says to Halim.

He gives her a smile. 'Sure thing, babe.'

After he has closed the door, Debra kicks off the shoes

and loses them in the back of the wardrobe for another week. She gives her feet a quick rub, slips on the old pair, and sits herself down at the dressing table before the next client arrives. She starts to brush her hair. Ali likes his girls to look groomed at all times, not like they've just been shagged through a hedge backwards.

Debra works the evening shift on Saturdays and she knows it will be a long night yet. The pubs have yet to close and that always brings a flock of clients in, all stinking of beer and sweat, or fags and sweat. On her black days she thinks life is just one long pounding to nowhere within a bad smell that never lifts.

She moves the brush over her hair, from crown to shoulder, in slow, sweeping arcs. In the mirror she inspects her reflection. Her hair looks golden in the lamplight and brushed until it shines.

Halim makes his way down a corridor, past three other closed doors, before he reaches the top of the stairs that will take him down into the reception area where two men sit around a coffee table. One of them is Halim's age. He sprawls across an armchair, chewing gum and watching football play on the portable TV. The other is much older. He flicks through the pages of one of the tattered girlie magazines that lie strewn about the table.

Ali sits at a desk in the corner, taking money, working the intercom and doing his bookkeeping in between the both. He doesn't talk to many of the punters, preferring to keep it business-like in case things get heavy. This being a Saturday he keeps things extra business-like. It is a rare Saturday when some problem doesn't come up that needs the inter-vention of his fists to sort out. Last week some creep left the front door hanging off its hinges after a scuffle on the doorstep. Cost him fifty quid to put right.

Ali scowls as he takes Halim's money, two twenty pound notes and one five. Halim tells him good night and Ali ignores him. He closes the money away in the desk drawer and goes back to doing his books. He keeps one eye out for the creep with the girlie mag who looks as if he might make trouble.

Outside, the night is cool and Halim turns the collar of his jacket up to keep out the chill. It is only a short walk home to where his son will already be asleep and Elif will be outstretched on the sofa, watching TV, with her swollen stomach high in the air looking like it's about to burst. He likes to treat Elif on payday and on the way back he will stop by the delicatessen and buy her baklava. He will wait until tomorrow before showing her the Nikes, until they are already on his son's feet before telling her how much they cost. Then she will be too taken with how cute their son looks and won't give Halim a hard time for not bringing enough money back this week. She never does ask where it goes. She never asks and he never tells. Instead he tells her not to worry. One day when he's running Abdi's shop he will be earning money enough. More money than they will ever know how to spend. Elif smiles. She lets herself believe him.

LESLEY GLAISTER

Rhinoceros

T HEY KISSED. She didn't even know his name. The kiss
was unexpected, unasked for, almost accidental.
Laughing at someone else's joke, they had both reached
for their drinks at the same instant, their faces seemed so
close there seemed nothing else to do but kiss, as if being so
close and not kissing would have been rude. It was a long,
soft and sizzling kiss. They pulled apart. His eyes glittering
at her in the smoky light. She was speechless, embarrassed
but unable to break his gaze. There was no intention there,
she thought, it was a spontaneous act, a spark lit, not quite
combustion.

Someone else spoke to her and she turned away and when
she looked back he'd gone. She blinked. I am a little drunk,
she thought, that was nothing, that was a stranger's kiss,
stop right there.

It was the penultimate night of a conference in Toronto.
Party night after five days of papers, seminars, discussions.
Her brain was tired but her body had woken up. Smoke
hung in the air and fogged round the wads of tobacco leaves
that dangled from the ceiling like sad Christmas decora-
tions. This was probably the only public place in Toronto
where smoking was not only allowed but encouraged. And
he had taken advantage, she had tasted it in his kiss. She
didn't smoke but was capable, it seemed, of smouldering.

She had another drink, got into a conversation about five-year olds, felt a deep pang thinking of her daughter, felt another as she glimpsed the profile of the almost-stranger. She tore her eyes away and forced her mind back on to the funny little things they say. At the end of the evening, as she was putting on her coat, he came up close behind her. She didn't turn, had no way of knowing it was him except the way all the cells in her body orientated themselves his way, like iron filings towards a magnet. She felt his warm breath on her skin as he leant in close to her ear. 'Zoo. Noon tomorrow,' he said. She said nothing, buttoned her coat, jammed on her hat, and left.

Back in her hotel room she stared at herself in the mirror. Mascara smudged under one eye, hat-flattened hair. She reeked shockingly of smoke in the bland, air-conditioned room. There was a message from John on the phone. He missed her; Nicky had won a prize for colouring-in; the cat had fleas again. To rinse away the smell of smoke she stood under the shower, head back, warm water cascading over her face and body. The shower gel smelled like green crushed leaves. The kiss happened at about 10 p.m., she calculated. Because of the time difference it wasn't yet 10 p.m. at home, therefore as far as John was concerned, it could not actually have happened. She crawled, still damp, between the flat white sheets. Too many glasses of wine, no dinner, only canapés. She felt hungry for something solid and wholesome, mashed potatoes perhaps. The sheets were cool against against the planes of her married body and her head swam. She closed her eyes.

A free day. There was a trip to Niagara Falls planned, lunch included, before the flight tonight. A treat for the delegates. As if we are children, she thought, needing some sweeties after some ordeal. The phone rang, a colleague telling her that breakfast was being served. She climbed from the tangled mess of sheets and drew back the curtains. It was a brilliant autumn – fall rather – day, the sky high and glassy blue. She looked down at the silent traffic pulsing along the street, looking at her own green wrist veins. Can anyone see me here? she wondered, naked woman at the hotel window. She lifted both arms, yawned as she stretched: if someone was watching, let them.

She should hurry, pack, leave her luggage in the lobby, have some breakfast, get on the bus. But she wasn't hungry yet, didn't want to see a waterfall or anything or anyone. She felt a small nag of guilt. Why didn't she ring John last night? She sat on the bed and keyed in their home number, though he'd still be asleep. She left a message: *Well done to Nicky, see you both tomorrow, lots of love, and oh, the flea spray's under the sink.*

As soon as she put the phone down it rang, making her start. She stared at it for three rings before she picked it up. Just someone telling her to hurry up, they were about to board the bus. She opened her mouth and discovered a lie waiting on her tongue. 'Not feeling well,' she said, 'tummy and head.' The morning after?' her colleague said and she agreed. It wasn't quite a lie, she could feel the aftermath of too much wine and there was still a taint of smoke in the air from last night's clothes – almost the taste of it on her lips.

What would she do instead? Be a tourist? She'd buy presents to take home for Nicky and John. Something extra for Nicky for being such a clever girl. She remembered the colouring competition, Nicky at the kitchen table, so carefully crayoning between the lines of the butterflies and bees, milky forehead furrowed, tongue pinched between her teeth.

She finished her packing, dressed and when she was sure

the coast would be quite clear, went down to the lobby and ordered a latté and a blueberry muffin. She kept her eyes down while she breakfasted, flicking through the tourist leaflets. She could visit the Sky Dome, or ride the elevator up the CN tower. She could take a ferry to Toronto Island, go to a museum or a gallery – or she could go to the Zoo. He won't have meant it or if he did he'd be sure to have regretted the suggestion, or perhaps forgotten. He was most likely on the bus to Niagara right now. She might even have misheard him. Could he have said 'you' and not 'Zoo'? It was just a kiss that's all, a silly accidental kiss.

The Zoo was almost empty, the air clear and cold. She snuggled into her long lamb-skin coat and hat. There was just one yellow bus outside and children clutching clip-boards and pens rushed past her in pairs, but otherwise there was no one about. What a harmless, blameless way to spend the day, an innocent pleasure, a solitary outing to the zoo. So good to be alone after a week of constant chatter and proximity.

She stopped to watch a group of warthogs scuffling in the dirt and wondered if he, at the Falls, would be wondering if she was here. Her face heated with the thought. What a fool he'd think her. But he would never know.

She shivered as an icy breeze riffled the yellow leaves around her feet. She went into the nearest building and gasped at the rich rank stench. Two rhinos stood on the far side of a murky green pool. Preposterous creatures, like some crazy inventions, with their dull, carved plates, log-shaped faces and minute prehistoric eyes. Their little tails fitted neatly in a dung-smeared groove between the plates and when they walked it was like old men in carpet slippers, a padded buffing on the concrete floor.

She watched them for a few moments, leaning her elbows on the barrier rail. She was about to leave and search out the great apes, when the door swung open.

'There you are,' he said.

'Preposterous,' was all she could think of to reply. She flushed and gestured at the creatures.

'Preposterous rhinoceros,' he said, taking her in. 'You came.'

She watched one of the rhinos butting its head against the wall.

'I wonder what the plural is,' she said. No use denying that she'd come. She turned back to face him and there he was with his stranger's eyes looking down into her own. His eyes were toffee brown, his black hair sprung with grey. She looked at the fine peaked edges of his lips.

'What?' he said.

'Rhinoceroses or rhinoceri?'

'Search me.' He brought his lips down on her own. Her mouth opened with surprise, tasting smoke overlaid with peppermint. Had he sucked a peppermint in preparation?

'Hannah, isn't it?' he said, releasing her.

She laughed. Two kisses and they'd never been introduced. 'And you are Paul?'

'That's me.'

They stared at each other and though it was warm in the rhino stink, her teeth began to chatter.

'You didn't fancy Niagara then?' she said.

His smile started at one corner of his lips and slid along. 'I didn't fancy *Niagara*,' he agreed.

Her treacherous married belly did a flip. She turned away.

'I haven't been to the zoo for ages,' she said, remembering with a pang the last time: with John on Nicky's second birthday. Nicky with her froggy wellies feeding the rabbits in the petting pen, her little fists stuffed with pellets.

'Nor me,' he said. 'I never thought you'd come.'

'I didn't, I mean I didn't necessarily think you'd be here,' she said. 'I just thought, zoo, nice day, nice idea.'

'Me too,' he said.

They left the rhinos behind, pushing out into the crisp blue air. She pulled her hat further down over her ears. It was icy, leaves skittered towards them like a swarm of mice.

'Shall we see the big cats?' he asked. 'I suppose you're married?'

'The tigers are over there,' she said, noticing the sign. 'Yes, I suppose I am. You?'

She looked up at him. His lashes were thick, and around his eyes a web of laughter lines. He shrugged, charmingly sheepish as he nodded. 'Kids?' he said.

They swapped the names and ages of their children – though not their spouses – as they watched a tiger prowl from one end of its enclosure to the other, and then flow upwards and stand high on a rock, gazing past them as it they were nothing, distance in its eyes.

'Beautiful,' she said, 'isn't that the most beautiful thing you've ever seen? It's so vivid, so,' she searched for a suitable word, 'so tigerish.'

'Burning bright,' he said, inevitably. 'Can we,' he was looking up at the tiger, 'I don't do this, honestly, but can we go back to the hotel? Get a cab?'

'I came by public transport.' She winced at the prissy sound of her voice. 'Let's see the gorillas first.' The hairs on her arms prickled towards him, she feared that if she took off her hat, her hair would flow out and wind around his arms. This was not a feeling she had ever had and this was not something she would ever do, something as corny as having a fling with an almost stranger on the last day of a conference, having a fling with the father of Alfie – who was the same age as Nicky almost to the day.

Fling, she thought, it sounds so careless and young. It sounds harmless.

He took her hand. The fine leather of her glove against the wool of his. His big strong fingers clasped her own. A different hand hold, John's was less insistent and their fingers always interlaced, friendly and loose, hands that knew each other. These fingers were tight and strange and sent quivers travelling up her arm.

'Gorillas first,' he agreed, 'and then we jump in the cab.' He pulled her against him, the buttons of his coat against her face. Taller than John and bigger altogether. She felt sheltered by his bulk.

As they pushed through the doors into the gorilla house, a trail of children came out, excited and shrieking, beating their fists against their chest. About the same age as Nicky – and Alfie. She looked up at Paul, was he thinking the same? But he met her eyes and smiled into them a way that told her no.

Behind the tall wire fence, the gorillas' enclosure had trees and caves, nets to climb, ropes to swing on – a little sample of gorilla heaven. Paul let go of her hand and removed his glove, then he took her hand in his and eased off her glove. She watched as his long fingers with the little black hairs on the backs and the clean, blunt nails, peeled the leather away from her skin. And then he held her naked hand in his and this time his fingers slid between her own, so snugly, so intimately, it took her breath away.

They were being watched. In the foreground of the enclosure a female gorilla squatted, regarded them with serious eyes while without looking away, she reached out and with a cushioned palm drew her baby to her breast. The baby opened its mouth, clamped on to her pendulous nipple and closed its eyes. Gorilla milk, she thought, how much like human? She felt, as she sometimes did watching another woman feeding a baby, a prickle of memory in her own breasts, a twinge of envy and nostalgia.

Nearby a gigantic silver-backed male – surely the alpha male – sprawled on the ground, drowsy, scratching delicately between his legs with long gentle nails. A young gorilla clowned with a red bucket, putting it over his head, loping a few yards and taking it off to see where he was. Hannah laughed. She wished Nicky was there to see.

'Seen enough?' Paul said, circling his thumb in the palm of her hand. 'Let's find a cab. We can be back in half-an-hour.'

The gorilla mother made her lips into a soft tube and grunted as she stroked the back of her child. Hannah met her eyes and flinched at the serious bright brown gaze. Something passed out of her like a breath. She looked down at the pale knot of clasped hands that hung between her and Paul, at his busily circling thumb.

The mother gorilla flicked Paul a look, got up, child dangling from her breast and loped away, the knuckles of her free hand scuffing the dust. Hannah removed her hand from Paul's and put her glove back on.

FRANCINE STOCK

Antechamber

D R PATTNI is in the hallway. She's bending forward to rub her hands with surgical scrub; she doesn't know I'm watching her through the little window. She's gazing ahead at the greenish white tiles and the sign that tells you to dispose of sharps and needles in the hazardous waste bin. The low light in the cubicle and the wire mesh in the glass blur the outlines of her face but I can still make out the slight bagging of the skin over her cheekbones, the swing of her hair before it winds back into the plait. Her ritual couldn't be more ordinary, but with only her head and shoulders visible, it looks mysterious, even dreamy. She leans forward with a little shrug, shutting off the taps with her forearms, like medics do, and turns my way. She's still looking down; I can see the grey stripe that runs from her parting. The door handle into my room presses down and suddenly she's here. Above the frill of the paper mask her eyes are serious.

'Hello, Sara,' she says slowly. The mask puffs out with her words, draws in with her breath. 'How are you today?'

Feet in white overshoes shuffle in all day, nervysidlingskaters, up to the side of the bed, but Dr Pattni glides. Senior doctors like her don't usually visit this time of the morning. Nurses do, physiotherapists, porters, cleaners. People who'll pass the time with a chat as if there were nothing better to do. But there isn't, is there?

I should know; I've tried all the ways God gives. Rabbit, rabbit. Sara who talks for England. I'm usually up for a rap; it's part of my job, what keeps me at the top of the bonus league. I'm a high-grade talker, but I have to admit in here the rules are different. Think about your working day. Think about mine for that matter. Sullen silence on the train, same old yadder in the coffee place, dozy e-flirtation, gossip by the water machine, bums perched on desks, sales-figuressextipsdietplans. Anything to keep going until six-thirty and the bar and in any case you can't hear a word there. In here, though, every word works double time.

I've had a bit of a make-over in my room, turned the cell into a chill zone. Dad brought in the lamps. Dr Pattni says it looks lovely after dark, my little temple, although on queasy chemo days, I switch the lava lamp off. All that spewing into glowing red plasma. I won't tell Dad that, not after he went all that way to the clearance shop.

The pin-ups aren't bad, though. There's the cat, of course, bless. But check out the pecs on the guys, those fab abs and the arms, I've got this thing for men's arms. There's a bit just above the elbow where it surges out, sand-dunesmooth. Beautiful. Great view out the window to the site down below. It's some extension for the hospital. Professor Zog's Cosmic Ray Therapy Unit or something, currently operating out of a disused Kit-Kat carton in a cupboard, but soon to be installed in hi-tech splendour and opened by the Queen, bugger me. It's like that advert, the guys on the site take a break at more or less the same time each day. There are a couple of fit ones, no more than a couple really because this *isn't* the advert, but they're nice-looking blokes with solid bodies, really well proportioned.

If I've got all my make-up on by then, I put on a bit of a show for them, waving and posing fullmetaljacket: wig du jour (blue today), eyelashes and nails. Fucking disco diva at 10 a.m., no wonder they all jump up and down. The window doesn't open, but through the double glazing I can just catch their shouts and they're well up for it, believe me. Little Barbie boys down among the sand and the cement. Just possibly, maybe tonight even, just before they give the girlfriend one, this little flash of blue might pass through the lustmist behind their lids. Hello, boys. What *am* I like?

But then again, if I'm not doing the foxy lady, if I haven't got the slap on, I don't bother much. I just put my earphones in, lie flat on the bed and drift off. There's always a choice.

I did think it might be fun to call them on the mobile, but you can't use it in here. Hiccuping pacemakers and zig-zags tearing across ITC monitors. Blimey. So I get on the steamphone and call my mate Lareesa down the corridor, so she can get to the window and wave too. She's my girlfriend, Lareesa, although we've never actually met face-to-face, opportunities being on the slim side in isolation. Maybe in a couple of weeks, when my white cells mosey back in, I could make faces at her through the little glass oblong in her door. In the meantime, she's just Hot Stuff, the Boiling Woman, Ms Raging Temperature. One night, early on, a couple of the housemen were in here poking around some nasty infection creeping around my line, the piece of plastic plumbing in my chest that connects my misbehaving blood to the outside world, the two-way valve that sucks in the dope, dispenses the juice. In between the tugging and the swabbing at the staphococcus, and me gazing into the eyes of the good-looking one, they started to crack these remarks about the girl down the hall. Not disrespectful, just amazed. For God's sake, they said, why isn't she dead yet? Her temperature's been at 44 degrees for five days, her organs must be frying.

That girl can scream, I tell you. At night I could hear her, roaring and griping like an extra on *Casualty*. At first, it put the wind up me. I like to make my own world in here, moody lighting, something soulful on the CD. When the lights twinkle out across the city, it could be a penthouse apartment. Then this woman down the hall sets up her moaning, like the Grim Reaper was scratching at her door. You don't think at first a din like that could be healthy, but the ones you have to worry about are the ones you don't hear, the ones slipping quietly into mucusunderworld – muscles soft, heartbeats slow. Lareesa was yelling out her rage, boiling over for real. Go, girl, I say. Her kind of people can stand high body temperatures but not the pain. She was just letting us know. The nurses got the joke. Ooh, they'd say, she does go on.

By comparison, I'm Ms Sunshine, though when I had a run-in with some bastard tummy microbe a week or so ago, I got really ratty. I was kicking-off, demanding the doctors. They scored me the top-rated, class A antibiotic, the drug of last resort when your immune system's down. Later, at so-called night, (there's no silence, no dark in a hospital; there's just eyelids slammed shut against neon glare . . . and ear-plugs) I began tripping. Characters swam up the walls; clamps and lamps weaved like snakes. Not frightening as such, cool and clear like video. I could have been at home, sleeping off a hangover on a Saturday morning – and the hospital, the cancer, could have been the REM sideshow.

Some isolation this is, like Piccadilly fucking Circus in here with that door swinging open every five minutes, temperature checks, blood, pee, the works. Everyone thought isolation would be torture for a party animal. They thought I'd go mental, stuck on my own in one little room, with just a shower and a bog for variety. They sent helium balloons the first day, the mad bastards. I attached them to the machines that delivered the chemotherapy, but it wasn't practical. To tell the truth, I got to hate those balloons. The shiny blue made me sick. And the red and the pink. It was the same with the DVDs I'd brought in, by the end of the first week all that colour and gloss seemed overcooked, like your aunty's frocks at Christmas, sticky and painful, nail-polish on a hangnail. Once, when I tried to get to the lav attached to all those balloons, I got tangled up in the strings.

So there I was, lying on the bloody bathroom floor, brought down by a balloon. I had to pull the emergency cord. The nurse came in. 'You OK?' he asked, raising a studded eyebrow. 'Ooops, I guess not.' And he hauled me up. I couldn't keep my eyes off the studs because at least two of them were inflamed, like zits, with little white heads. Ah, I said, white cells, right? Lucky you. That's what I said, anyway, but I thought what the *fuck* is going on? Infection? In my so-called sterile environment? Oh, please. I don't want some poxy spot messing up my chances. The cancer's a respectable high-tech action-type foe. You don't want to be carried off by a pickpocket.

Mum had noticed the studs, naturally, when she'd been in earlier. She'd looked at me, sharpish, like an accusation, as if I'd somehow encouraged them with my wigs and my nail-art and the diamond-studded false eyelashes. I love my mum, don't misunderstand me, but these last weeks I bloody hate it when she's around. With Dad, it's so much easier. Mum, stop staring at me. Stop looking at the charts and asking me to jump on the scales. Stop pumping me for good news. Nobody can give you what you want right now, especially not me. Cut me some slack. If I said that, though, she'd probably develop stigmata to match her nail varnish. I can't bear it when she purses her upper lip into furrows and tries to talk about something else, because she can't hold out for long. Surely, she says, surely if they say you might be out in three weeks, your blood counts must be up?

When Dad's in here, he sits there hystericalduckyfeet playing with one of those puzzles people give you, knots and rings and little plastic discs with curvy lines on them that – put together right – make a perfect pattern, Celtic like the tattoos. The kind of pattern you can't ever get out of, the kind God, if he does exist, might look like. Dad knows I can't reassure him, that I've got enough to do. He's just carrying on as if I'm having my tonsils out. He's a bit of an ostrich, my dad. Fine by me.

It's still great when my mates phone, of course, but their voices are high and nervy, like they've just been caught doing something bad and when they visit, they sit there tidymouseyhyperclean, hairsprayed brides in photographers' windows. They don't laugh at the insane things that happen in here. Sometimes, especially when they've just given me the steroids, I can't stop the spiel. And then they say, Sara, you're mad as a fox, just like normal. You daft bitch, what are you like? But their eyes are a bit glazy and they keep looking round at stuff, all suspicious. Like there's something wrong with it, when it's *my* stuff, my machines, my pills in their little plastic trays. I'm quite attached to those drugs now. The pills with the dozing eyes for sleep, the yellow ones and the mauve ones to fight the sickness or give me the munchies.

When they've gone, it's almost a relief. It's like they're the *Star Trek* team going back on board, while I'm the Alien

Queen, who's snogged the captain, but decides at the end of the episode to stay on her electric blue planet. I'm breathing the blue planet air, here in the duck-egg blue cell, with the shiny painted walls. And I'm doing well; in fact, I'm thriving, like an exotic space plant, with my talons and my long wig. I need this environment. When someone comes in from Earth, they disturb it. Maybe it's the chemotherapy: nothing tastes the same any more – it's all extreme. It's too much salt or sweet or acid. My taste buds can't cope. Like the videos or the TV or the radio, all those people talking about nothing, talking without knowing. Sometimes, my mates spout this bollocks about me winning, how they know I'll be back soon to rejoin the team. Or worse, they try to talk about 'feelings' like you buy them in Claire's Accessories. Or the 'pain' of losing my hair. What is this, fucking Oprah? I just think, don't try and make deals with me, get a life.

Anyway, it's all entertainment here, like the huge woman with the test-tubes who visits at six forty-five each morning. Vampire Lady. It's her privilege to find me before the wig and make-up, in my film diva turban. She perches her enormous arse on the bed and settles in for a laugh. Her hands move like a cardsharp: I hardly feel her turn the tap on the tube in my chest and siphon off a few mils of gore. Umm, lovely, she smacks her lips. Look at that. Then she labels it up and pops it in its own little socket in her tray, which she pushes around the place scaryairhostess. She makes jokes too, about the care-home she went to and her little brother with his foster family, and the long slog to the exams. She rolls to the door, the little pigtails at the end of her cornrows sticking out like some cartoon kid. Then she waves without looking back, squeezing the trolley through the door. Her trolley carries little bits of me that don't belong to me any more down to the labs where they turn into crosses and lines on my graph. It's a weird deal: I reckon she performs a kind of secret transfusion, myself, when she takes the blood. I think she puts something else in, something lightsweetheadybacardibreezer. I feel better after she's been, anyway.

All my visitors go through that little ante-room. They dress up; they undress. They're in, they're out of my life. Even my room is an antechamber. Might be getting out soon. Might be staying in. An antechamber always has two doors.

God's Representative arrives at two. Mum took it upon herself to put the RC on my form. Being arsey? said Dad. *I* see, I said. RC, indeed. Mum looked upset and a little shifty. Dad and I had you christened, she began, so that perhaps one day . . . and then she trailed off. Well, what? I said. (Get yourself out of that, Mum.) Well, you're not *nothing*, she said in the end, you have to be *something*. Thanks, Mum, I said. And Dad and I smirked, like little kids.

So now, after lunch every day, a head bobs into view in the little window. It's a small head, with dark hair that manages to be fluffy and greasy at the same time. It keeps its eyes down, concentrating on the scrubbing, tying the plastic ties on the apron carefully, squeezing on the polythene galoshes. Then there's a fumbling with the door handle and slowly it shambles in, wonkysportsjacketshinytrousers-flipperfeet.

Father Mark pulls up the little metal frame chair, never the upholstered one, and sits at right angles to me, so he doesn't have to look me in the eye. So, he sighs, and how are you, Sara? Fine, of course, I chirrup. Or not so good today, or could be better. Sometimes I throw him these little tidbits.

Now, I don't know what kind of training these guys have, but I always thought (and films have a lot to answer for here) that a priest's visit should involve a reassuring hand on the wrist, or an invitation to reflect together on life, or maybe *even* a nanosecond of prayer. You know, just a little 'Our Father' or something. I might even dredge up a Hail Mary myself, except for that bit about the hour of our death. Some days I'm so up on account of the drugs I'd go for it. I feel like saying, 'Father, is there something I could do for *you*?' He's probably uttered twenty words, no more, in all his visits. That's like a ratio of two thousand to one: minutes spent robing up for isolation unit versus time spent pastoral caring. Sighs a bit, though, in a sort of spiritual, sympathetic way. Better than that creepy massage guy and his visualizations, anyway.

Which is where Dr Pattni comes in. Not literally, not now, not in the way she's walking so slowly towards the side of the bed, not in the way she's tidying the tassels on one of my cushions as she watches two Barbie-men down on the site slot a steel joist into place. No, Dr Pattni makes an appearance here because her conversations are like white gold and diamonds or the moment you realize the DJ has heard of soul.

She frightened me at first. Even though she doesn't seem that old, there's the grey stripe in her hair and that long solemn face. When she came with the consultant, the chippy one with the denim shirts, she kept in the background and never, ever, smiled.

Once, though, she dropped by in the afternoon and I was crying. I don't do it much, but I was just so hacked off with the machines and the drugs and this tap in my chest and the metallic taste and not being able to get away, just for an hour, from the hospital, from the blood results, from the prognoses and the charts and the watchful looks. I miss my cat, I offered. True, but not, in this case, the truth.

She told me a little about what she knew of missing things. About the children she left behind with her parents in Kenya, while she came to this country to study. About the way the telephone system didn't work and how she didn't have enough money to call home. She said she used to have nightmares about her little ones having accidents, about bicycles running into them, or fire licking through the kitchen, snakes under the table, scorpions in the shower: she was forever afraid she could never get there in time. How old are they? I asked. In those days, she said, they were babies, but my daughter has just qualified in Bristol. Oh, she added, like an apology, as a doctor.

Her eyes were just a little bit shiny and that made me cry all over again: for the times that she never got there; for her giving up seeing them toddling for the right to work in this crumbling shit-coloured hospital under London drizzle-sludge. I felt proud and sad. I hardly know the woman, but things are now so bright and close when before they were sealed off, like those see-through covers people put on their sofas. I love Dr Pattni because she's not scared of me, or what might happen to me. She doesn't see me in an antechamber: she just looks at me, not up, not down, no patientdaughtersaint deal, just straight.

I told her about Father Mark and his silent ministry and we laughed. You know, she said, looking out the window, where the avocado river was gleaming and the City towers (my towers) were polished sexy, I'm not a religious person in any formal way. And not indeed, in any way at all for many years. But when I began to specialize in haematology, I found patterns in blood cells, wonderful patterns, geometrical, symmetrical, that filled me with amazement and a kind of respect. I would return to them and marvel at their structure. They really took my breath away. I don't worship a single god, Sara, but I believe in, I don't know, the wonder of the body, of the cells. The architecture of the blood. And she touched me then, which they don't do normally, unless it's for a pulse, and she traced along the vein on the inside of my wrist, beside the little puncture marks from the catheters. Beautiful, she said.

Even when it goes wrong? I said.

Go wrong, she said, isn't a term we use, Sara. You should know that by now. We talk about variation. Cells reproduce faster or fail to thrive. They find ingenious new forms. Sometimes, they're being wonderfully clever, finding ways to survive. No right; no wrong.

Before I came in here, I thought there was. In my conversations with doctors, I was looking for the 'right' answer, checking their eyes for the sign that said 'Way Out'. Thanks for your help, I'll be getting along then. But I've been down so many corridors since, I'm learning there's no point in asking. Sometimes, it's more than OK to come back to some place you've been before, like this ward. Just for a while.

When you're a kid, you think, if I do all right in the maths test, then everything will be fine. And you bugger it up, and it's still OK. But you don't stop thinking like that. Everyone thinks it about me. People want you to fall into one category or another, this door or that. Will she live? Will she die? Does she have a positive attitude? Did her lifestyle contribute? I hate that. It makes out that *I'm* not important. Funnily enough, I'm not the victim, or the heroine here, you shouldn't admire me, or pity me. I'm not the brave warrior of the Tribe of the Sick, the tribe you don't belong to. Yet. I haven't won or lost. I'm not cured, but I'm not doomed either. I'm not the slut or the goody-goody. I'm not salt and no way am I sweet. Yet I'll bet you've already made assumptions. You want to know if you were right to invest your time in me, whether my little hospital story is poignant or inspiring.

Just listen to this. While you're judging and weighing and pondering, at least I know what I'm doing. I'm living, every bit as much as you, more so in fact, when I least expect it, smiling in the shit, the human thing, which no other animal can manage. Touching in the real sense, not like Julia Roberts expiring onscreen weepygulpybigeyes but Vampire Lady telling her brother my knock-knock joke dead straight. A flash of blue behind some guy's half-closed lids. Dr Pattni's finger on my skin, her loss of her children's baby years God knows how many decades ago bringing water to my eyes. Children I don't know, places I haven't been firing inside me as if they were mine. No history, no form, no track record, just from her to me, freely given. That's the moment. That. The business.

And so this is Dr Pattni now, really now, and she's turning from the window and taking that step over to the bed. She sinks down, pushing her plait back over her shoulder. She has a piece of paper in her hand, which I hadn't noticed before. It has graphs and ratios and curves, the plans and elevations of my blood.

I am talking away to her. You know what I'm like.

'Sara,' she says, 'Sara, listen. I have something to tell you.'

HANNAH
MURGATROYD

In the Forest, In the Field

T HERE IS that place in dreams which is a step beyond the world you know. In your sleep you stand in an empty parking lot edged by woods. In the dirt-darkness shopping carts lie abandoned, small creatures live, pederasts lie in wait. If you walk forward into the trees the world will segue into dream and you will sense the familiar but you won't know all the directions and part of you will be aware that this is a world that does not exist.

I was born on the prairie, in the light of a falling star. The wind whipped into wheat and I was creamy and yellow, a child of the soil and the sky. My mother always walked me home from school. When my father threw me up in the air and ran with light spirit, I was the envy of all.

We moved to White Pines in February. Another quick and badly-built development similar to the houses subsiding by the river, saggy-roofed and shambling as silt beds suck them down in the slowest ever quicksand. Up on the hill here these box-frames fear they'll puff away in dryness, all the nutrients in the earth ploughed back under the tarmacadam. Our old home was sited a few yards down and all the fields around our garden, suiting my father, a wildlife painter. But we didn't own the land, it was bulldozed away from us and we could not prevent it.

In the kitchen my sister Merry's slip jimps across her body, undecided on which lovely mound to settle. She is all mumpfaced, mouth switched inward and eyes ablast with darkness under her brow. If I was a man I would love her right here and now. She's an earthen shade caused by her home-tanning lamp and highlit by all the white of the walls and she rubs her fingers on her crepy forearm like the rushing of brown leaves.

'Merry?'

She won't look at me. There is this thing that has made us all wrong this summer so we'll drink and drink and we'll sleep and we'll walk hard-assed, eyes shut.

Merry used to be dynamite, two months ago. She had all the charm of disaffection and premature laying-downs sweetened with a kitten's twitchiness and soft appeal. She cut hair and painted nails and laughed at how dumb salon girls are whilst applying her own perfect French manicure. These days she constantly creams her hands, they appear drier with each treatment. Mostly I walk in and see her laying on the polish and five minutes later removing it, buttering her hands, filing, buffing, painting on the base, blow, application one, blow, application two, blow, clear top coat, blow. Her cigarettes are ready shaken out on the table, the beer uncapped so that nothing messes each drying layer.

Drinking is there to fill holes. Once holes are topped with liquid they overflow, you find you are stood with great geysers of foamy beer shooting out of arms and chest and head. Everyone in this family has holes in their buckets. I want to ride horses properly fast and throw knives but I don't, I get drunk.

Our houses squat on the brow of a field, the dirt lifts off in clouds like sea spray where crops no longer root. In the far distance, a railroad track, one or two trains a day and they don't care to hoot us. There are fourteen timbered houses on the snaking White Pines road, all garage doors shut and cars at work or being washed on driveways, fresh laid like liquorice belts. Everyone of us has mailboxes, candle pines, a basketball hoop and a hundred songs of sad and happiness if you cross on to our porches.

I go down the road with my hooded top pulled tight round my ears and run with my arms crooked up, like a jogger, so I appear normal. The neighbourhood is sunny and other girls are in summer dresses and I am pickled in my sweat top, briny with hops and heat.

'Hey!'

Smack smack go my tennis shoes.

'Hey! Eileen!'

Smack smack smack smack.

'You fucking weirdo.'

And I stop. I don't turn, yet, but my arms are high like a cocky featherweight and sweat rivers down my hamstrings. Each blade of grass beats its neighbour, a beetle climbs a tip then falls off, someone snippets furiously at their box hedge. Now girls generally don't punch someone out, they hair pull and kick and scratch at most. I, however, am drunk and have a cavity where giving a shit used to room. I ran that off when my mother died and I'm still grieving. I turn.

'You want some?'

Elizabeth Dutch has a giggle caught in her throat like a cock and she chokes.

'Nut-nut,' she says, tapping on her skull.

I advance. Her gloss lips wrap a sneer around small

incisors, I will wipe it off. She glides across the lawn with three lesser girls beside.

'Lesbian,' she snickers.

Smack. Shrieks. Elizabeth goes down. Leaning over I see a little blood spattering her posy-sprigged dress. Turning my fist I see my knuckle is pink with her lipstick.

'It's all right, Elizabeth. Guys don't like to feel teeth when you suck them off.'

I run, fast, more through exhilaration than fear of being caught. I haven't felt this good all summer.

On the street there are faces who do not look and mouths that do. On the street there are hands that reach out and fingers that ensnare my own little fears that jump in my throat and clamour for the top of the world's attention. It was horrible, horrible, the death.

When I walked as a child with Daddy on the street, it was slow, his stick timing out steps as we progressed with his hand on my small shoulder. He was like an army greatcoat, huge, comforting, a staid shell of dignity and he smelled as worn and as spring green and as mud green. I see him at the bottom of the road, a bag full of bottles weighing his body unequal and he stumbles. He has a lump on his head from passing out last week. I pull my hood tight and run fast back towards the house. He leans on a new stick (hospital issue, grey plastic moulded handle, pitted metal, rubber tip) and watches me skit away. At home there is a tub plenty with sticks: Scottie dog heads, big beaters for pushing back brambles, hollow polished staffs hiding nips of whisky. Dad always had a funny leg but he never used an invalid's stick. My mother would have killed him.

I know the boy who did it. His name is Nate and he took the hunting rifle down from the kitchen wall where his father had hung it since before he was born and went into the fields heavy with grass. The papers write he is an outsider, nobody spoke to him. Nobody speaks to me either and I know right from wrong. This boy, sometimes I have a class with him and he's stupid, like a soft-boiled egg. He sits at the back all tall, like a bus stop pole, and hums and laughs at punch lines when no one told him the joke. He licks his hair down to flatten it and is stupid because he wants to belong. His name is Nate and he kidnapped our childhood.

Someone has trimmed the lawn. It must be Merry. Dad is not one of those men who water and tend their grass more frequently than their own children. In April Mom seeded flowers from a packet with her arm outstretched, spinning a circle and they still flourish meadow-like with dippy heads in cherry, citrus stripe and milk. I wonder if the man next door admires such anarchy. His wife's rockery resembles a demolished quarry, the brave young heathers and rock roses stand no chance against this mountain range of rubble. The importance of order on these turf subdivisions still confounds us, having never lived so close by people. We own no matching garden furniture and we open our windows opposing the dry wheeze of air conditioning. They considered us freaks even before Mom died.

'Merry?'

'Get your bathing suit on!'

Indoors Merry is moving in an orange bikini with grass clippings basted to her sun-oiled legs. Her nails must be dry because she's rooting through the refrigerator like a hog on heat, slinging anonymous vacuum packs into the cool box. She knocks the assorted fridge magnets to the floor and the kitchen whirrs with unusual energy, paper memos floating out the door like sheets on washing day. Goodbye to lists of things to buy and funeral home receipts and soap powder coupons and unanswered letters from tabloid talk shows and my school asking if I'm ever going back.

'Shift it Eileen, we're going to the lake.'

'Oh. Are you sure? I've got . . .'

'You've got nothing to do. Come on.'

She rolls me out the door into the car, ambushing my father as we pass. In three seconds we're in the white Oldsmobile with its burgundy plush interior, Merry at the wheel. This car has always reminded me of a casket, swagged in silk and suffocating with the windows rolled up. We should have had a rosary and a plastic Jesus on the dashboard instead of the faded copy of *Birds Of Nebraska* and some opera eyeglasses. Merry burns it out of town. Taking a bottle from the bag Dad says to her whilst staring at an abstract point of sky, 'You shouldn't drive drunk.'

'I'm not,' she says, 'I'm just merry,' laughing at her joke.

When the police released the body we had Mom cremated. There was no one she could have endured lying next to in the cemetery. It was a private ceremony, just the three of us, and a week later we collected her in a bronze plastic pot with a big screw lid. It resembled the jugs of kosher chicken bouillon she insisted on buying because 'the Jewish know how to make good chicken soup'.

'She shouldn't all fit in there,' Merry had said, putting her up on the kitchen shelf.

'It's not much of an urn, looks more like a picnic flask – careful you don't pour coffee in it' I'd replied.

She stayed on the bookshelf overlooking each of our meals together, propping the space between the *National Geographic* stack and *Vietnam: A History*. Most evenings before I sleep I sneak in and say goodnight, sometimes I unscrew the lid and whisper *I love you* to the grey dust, half-hoping one day it'll take form and whisper it back.

Occasionally there seems less of her, perhaps Dad or Merry have been pinching her for their own private ceremonies. Once upon a time we would have scattered her on this land. Now the ashes would catch in other people's screen doors like a sieve or stick to the rubber of their car tyres. Perversely I wish to go ahead and do it anyway, then tell them and watch the fear grab their eyes, afraid they may have swallowed a dead person, afraid her spirit is rested in their gardens. There are no touchable memories of my mother here, all I can see is her arguing with Dad, a hot pink spot on each cheek, *Just sell the goddamn house, Bill, I hate living here.*

The lake is empty. It's a week after Labor Day. We picnic on salami, crackers and mayonnaise. We smoke cigarette after cigarette to rid our mouths of the greasy flavour.

'I hit someone today.'

Even my father looks up, his eyes a-flicker.

'Who?'

'Elizabeth Dutch. I think I broke her teeth.'

'It's okay,' says Dad. 'Her father's an orthodontist.'

'Yep,' concurs Merry, 'And you're half an orphan now. You can get away with murder.'

The lake pools out undisturbed and windless like mirror glass. Tree stumps and dumped concrete threaded with rusty metal spokes stick out where the levels have dropped. There are dehydration lines on the bank and I wouldn't swim in it, the water never moves, it simply gets heavier with people's leavings.

Merry produces the jar. To call it an urn suggests something ancient, Greek or Roman, terracotta even.

'I brought Mom along.'

'I guess she doesn't get to go on picnics now.'

'Duh. I meant I thought we could scatter her.'

'Here?'

'It's as good a place as any.'

'I sent some of her,' Dad says.

'Where to?'

'Poland. That's where her family came from. I didn't have a destination so I sent it Care of Poland.'

'Hope you didn't put a return address. They might have thought it was anthrax.'

Merry opens the jar.

'Don't waste it all,' I say. 'This isn't the best place.' I want to keep some of her at home.

'At least it's outside.'

Dad looks away from the lake to the horizon. 'She'll get carried from here on the pollen and wind. She can go anywhere she likes now.'

A father is generally a tall man. He does not have a limp and he has friends, male and female. In the night my father bumps into furniture and opens doors to find empty rooms and caves of closets where his shirts grow larger. The wood strapped to the house has no memory of breathing yet it accompanies his walk, stretching and sighing as it settles in the foundations. The walls are stuck crazily with his paintings big and small, of ducks, marshes, mink and scattered beechnuts to remind us of the good things still to be found where no people are. In his room grouse fly out of a culvert, whooping cranes migrate across the dresser and a grey wolf guards the door, silently padding in blue-lit snow. Each night Dad lies in the bed we were conceived in – in a living house, from an old other time – disappearing under the red star quilting stitched by his mother. I fix him coffee for breakfast with a brandy peep in. It shouldn't be normal but it is.

He takes a handful of the ashes and lets her go on the

breeze blowing away from us. Merry and I do likewise. The grey filaments tunnel out and disappear. The air lightens and a white butterfly lands on Merry's shoulder. She stretches back like a marmalade cat warming in the sun. Dad rolls over and rests, you don't know his leg is wonky when he lies down.

Then I see him. Nate. Stood over the lake watching us as if he was always there. He is still as a stripling in the shadow of mature trees, their full leaves huddle his form in protection. He shouldn't be there.

There are two local police officers, one of which is Nate's father. He was the one who entered the yard after it had happened where we were barbecuing steak and mixing potato salad, moderately happy. My father stood wearing a joke, a naked fat lady apron, holding a spearing fork like an unconfident first date with a red rose while the beef caught fire behind him. Over and over he murmured, 'I don't believe you.'

'I'm sorry. I'm so sorry.' Is all Nate's father could reply.

'My wife is dead you say. Who shot my wife?'

'My son.'

Three pairs of uncomprehending eyes screwed up against the sunlight. The questions rolled over and over but the answers couldn't quite fit. 'How old is he?'

'Seventeen.'

'And why did he have a gun?'

'It's my hunting rifle. I taught him to shoot. He's a good shot.' The policeman started to cry and wandered away. We drove to the mortuary to identify the body. We drove to the field where my mother had been walking. She'd asked if any of us had wanted to accompany her. Merry and I were reading trashy magazines, Dad was sleeping in the sun. The field was taped off, a crime scene but the guard had gone home so we crept in. The police had beat a path direct to the middle where there was a body-shaped collapse of grass. There was some brown where blood had stained but most of it had been soaked into the soil which was still wet, I touched it, to be sure. There had been no portentous thunder cracks or blue skies blacking seven hours before. We hadn't noticed when she died. When it began to drizzle we drove home and sat immovable staring out at the yard where the potato salad collected water and the charcoal fizzled out.

After he shot the stranger Nate went home and waited for his father with the rifle across his lap. He calmly told him what had occurred. Officer Munro checked the gun. One bullet had been fired. He made his son take him to the field then got on the radio, calling for help.

'Officer Munro . . . Walt Munro. I need an ambulance, it may be too late, there's a woman shot . . . I'm in the top field, north of Abraham, John Beaumont's land. The suspect is apprehended.'

The TV stations broadcast his appeal when they were alerted the next day. Five media vans greeted us that morning, pencil skirted ladies stood in our mother's Cosmos patch, microphones as big as their pleasantly smiling heads. Merry pulled the drapes and unplugged the phone, letting the neighbours make up answers to their retarded questions. I watched a few news bulletins, live footage shot outside the murder victim's house as her family grieved inside. If I had walked out the front door I would have appeared on screen. Everyone had their cameo moment, Nate in a natty orange jumpsuit, shackled and head bowed, Officer Munro in a daze, on repeat saying 'I always taught my son to respect guns, to value life. He's not a killer. He's not a natural killer.' Aerial shots of the field turned it as abstract and meaningless as a crop circle. Kids we didn't know at school got their fifteen minutes, their tears accompanied by a counselling hotline sailing across the screen. The media got hold of a family snapshot and they misappropriated its meaning. We became a headline, a montage of images: Teen Killer Tears Apart Perfect Family Now United In Grief. Losing our identity made us fall apart. Being cut adrift by this same media when they discovered a more interesting double suicide and a spate of stolen pet stories made us wish not ever to be put back together again.

There is the lake then there is Nate. He is standing under the biggest tree. It is a cottonwood. In the gold cast light the trunk is superb, like a great hand of God reaching up through the scrub to cast out the wicked, heal the sick. It is a solidified eruption of maple syrup and he is small beside it. Beyond Nate are the trees, then the parking lot, then the supermarket, then all the houses. I work the strings on my hood tight and turn my back – how can he be there?

Dad speaks from the ground.

'The trouble is I don't know how she wants us to behave,' (all these days spent perspiring in the smell of wine vats), 'We never discussed death.' He'd been close to it when his helicopter crashed in Vietnam. Tiny puckers of metal remain in his leg which he rubs whenever lightning strikes in the distance.

'We should sell up,' he says.

There are no grandparents or aunts or uncles who might bring us clean washing and home-baked casseroles and guide Dad. We go out unchecked and malfunction repeatedly, a factory line of spare parts missing the core, the tick in the tock. We are a mandolin without strings awaiting the pluck that makes the sense of our being and creates happy song.

'There'll be money you know, compensation if we want to sue.'

'How much?'

'In the thousands. A court would be sympathetic. Two girls with no mother, a devoted father, a gun-crazy adolescent.'

I close my eyes. I think about the forest floor Nate is standing on, a carpet of discarded confections. Turkey bones, roof insulation, yoghurt cups, a squashed grey sandal, always damp and scurried with biting ants and holes to turn your ankle in. The noise and real light hang suspended in the furthermost tops creating a dizzying cascading tent of silence under which you huddle. Each divine twilight finger streams in in accusation at what is hiding in the leaves, secrets dodge the sun like vampires and are shift-shapers, yielding up on occasion a dead cat, a condom packet or the lunch bag of a missing child. Birds camouflage their plumage and baby animals forage in safety not knowing time isn't limitless, there are mechanical diggers longing to penetrate the unopened ground.

'Why didn't the boy just go shoot a rabbit? Why a person? Why her?'

There is a silence. Nate has never volunteered why, the hardest part is accepting it was a motiveless act.

'Because he could.'

'He would have got away with it. She'd only have been found when Beaumont took his cattle up.'

Perhaps it would have been better not to know the killer's face, we could have given him the identity of a stalker, a spurned lover, a serial murderer. Not a boy, not this pathetic, ineffectual creature unfairly given all the power of God. Dad lets out a long breath and I would like to lie in the crook of his elbow and whisper I can see him, the killer, he is watching us.

'I thought I'd found the best and safest place for my girls here. We might as well live next door to thieves and crack whores, it's done us no good.'

Merry sounds out like a prophet. 'One day the rain will wash these rotten houses into matchsticks and these people won't matter. They don't matter now.'

Send them a flood. We want Dad to be our Noah.

I stand up decisively and face the lake, ready to shout and flap at Nate like I'm scaring the crows. A deer breaks cover and runs out across the field. I am stupid, in its stealth and watchfulness I mistook the animal for Nate.

Dad stirs. 'Let's go eat at a restaurant, we could all do with some real food.'

He puts an arm on my shoulder to rise and gives Merry his stick, arms cloaking our shoulders as he steadies himself between us. It'll be all right, I say, under my breath, clutching the urn to my breast.

'Eileen,' Dad says, fixing me then my sister with the hope willing fierce in his eyes, 'it will. One day soon it will all be all right.' He hasn't looked straight at us for weeks.

As we step from the lake out of a scant patch of yellow silphium a late plover bursts leading the way forth as it joins others to migrate. Bad memories are pretty much like hangovers, like dogs, you throw sticks at them and they keep dementedly returning, wagging tails, branches in mouth. Eventually they get tired and the sun goes down and they curl up in their basket in the corner and peace and you find a truce, however temporary. If you stop chucking drinks down your hatch like nickels and dimes the hangovers lessen. If you stop feeling pain you won't forget your mother. Pain should be allowed to migrate like birds, returning only when the weather is more clement or you have your raincoat on. It will come back a better, sharper, happier pain which makes allowances for weeping and uncertainty. The more a sadness comes and goes, the less afraid you become of a world that doesn't care or of the awfulness of people or of the bare fact that the best thing about life is missing from it for ever.

LUCY LEPCHANI

The Monarch

I AM BLINDFOLD with a Virgin Airways sleep mask and a soft, fleece scarf tied over that. My sister Emily tied it on carefully as we left the car, now about two hundred metres back down the road. We have climbed an easy fence, walked up a grassy slope past some trees that rustled softly in a tendril of September breeze, and then across a field of ankle-high grass. It is the softer, dusty green grass of northern California, near Mendocino. I know only that much, and that although I trust Emily and James, this is not my choice of fun. The air is warm but slightly breezy; I can smell the land and it smells of warm earth, of late summer, of early evening. Birds streak fast echoes in nearby sky. I feel its blue liquid light pour on to my skin. I stumble. Emily holds my right arm, which is linked through her left, her other hand reassuringly on my bicep. My left hand grips the black canvas bag that contains our father's ashes, close to my body. Emily's husband James grips me softly but firmly by that elbow.

'Hey! Nearly there Mikey!' he says, and I can tell he is smiling his wide, beach-boy smile.

'Wherever "there" is.' I reply, trying to sound happy about it. These are the only people on this planet I would trust to blindfold me and lead me into the unknown hills of a foreign land.

'Oooh, yes,' said Emily, 'wherever "there" might be. It could be . . . *anywhere*,' she whispered the word like a secret.

'I can't believe you're doing this, Em. I've flown the Atlantic to be bushwhacked by my own family.'

'Wrong continent,' she replied, 'bushwhacked is Australia. You're being corralled. Good old American ab-ducted!'

'And your father and your sister planned this last time he was here.'

'So he told me,' I replied, feeling the sadness of his recent passing begin to seep into my gut again, 'which is the only reason I'm here with you bandits.'

'Yeah!' said James through his grin. 'Bandidos! Watch out gringo!'

We had come to a halt, and Emily had let go of me. I heard her undoing the small backpack she carried, pull out the rug I had seen her put into it earlier. James let go of my arm. I stood there in the time-shifts of air, clutching the ashes of our dead father. Apparently, for a very good reason.

'Do you know which one this is, lad?'

'*Morpho didius*, Dad.'

'Cor-*rect*. And this one?'

'*Morpho Menelaus*.'

'Cor-*rect*. And this?'

'*Morpho Selene*.'

He closed the butterfly book and passed it across the pile of others on the table.

'Now Michael; common names, British butterflies. What's this one?'

'Red Admiral.'

'This?'

'Brimstone.'

'This?'

'Chalkhill blue.'

One by one I named the butterflies in the pictures, some of which I had learned to identify only the evening before, from the same book, and some of which were almost as familiar as my family. Dad's eyes twinkled with delight; he loved it when I got things right.

'Well done, lad. Well done. Do you know, when I was a boy in India, some of these butterflies were exotic to me. Now they're all over the bloody place! Annie, he got them all right, isn't that good?'

'Mmmm, lovely,' said my mother, more interested in the pages of her Mills and Boon novel, 'perhaps he could have some pocket money to go to the shops.'

She was near the end of the book, and we all recognized the expression, the posture, the small flicker of her steely grey eyes as they beamed into the pages. It meant: 'Do not disturb me. Interrupt at your peril.'

'Half-a-crown,' said Dad 'and yes, you can spend it all on sweets if you like. Just don't worry about your teeth all falling out, at least you know all your butterflies.' Dad, proud and awkward gave me the coin he fished from his pocket.

'Can you get some shopping too, Michael?' said Mum, in a distant, faraway tone. 'Give him a fiver, Viknesh, there's a list in the kitchen.'

'A fiver? How much shopping you bloody want him to get?' and Dad walked out of the room. I stood before Mum, uncomfortably turning over the half a crown in my hand. She looked up at me briefly and smiled, then turned back to her book.

'Will my football kit be ready for Monday, Mum? I put it

in the wash yesterday eve . . .' She interrupted with a loud sigh, and without looking up from the page said:

'Yes, yes.' And she was back in the arms of her fantasy hero once again.

'There's a whole weekend's shop here. He can't bloody carry all of this by . . .'

'Yes he can.'

'We'll drive to the supermarket. Doesn't look like we'll be doing much else this bloody weekend, does it?'

Mum didn't answer, or even look up at Dad. She turned a page gracefully.

'Get your jacket, Michael. You have to help me. Come on, let's go.' Dad took his jacket from the peg in the hall and turned to leave the house. He was angry, but he was letting it boil down rather than up. Mum, she was like ice. I knew she was angry but I didn't know why, but the fact that she held it inside her, poised and brittle, scared me. We got into the car quickly, and then drove through the streets to the town; Saturday traffic snared us in. Dad let out a sigh.

'Why's Mum not speaking to you Dad?'

His eyes flickered several blinks at once but his expression remained unchanged, and he didn't answer. I was just pondering whether to ask again, and he said softly:

'She's angry with me.' Dad sounded the horn at a driver who pulled across him, wound down the window and swore more than ever, but the other car drove on without response.

'You know Michael, sometimes we do things that seem at the time like the only thing to do. Like that idiot in that car that just pulled out – he took a risk or he'd have been stuck in that side road all day. He knew it was wrong, but he just had to do it. And it made me angry; well, in the same way, I've made your mother angry.'

'But what did you do Dad?'

'I lost all our savings on a horse. Bloody donkey.'

'Oh.' It was not the first time I had heard him say that, of course, but usually, Mum would shout and throw things, break the crockery on purpose – a terrible thing to my mind. But this time she was holding it all inside her, like an unexploded bomb. Very scary.

The Maytime sun shone outside, and the car was beginning to feel hot, despite the open windows; the atmosphere inside the car seemed clammy and dull by contrast.

'There's something else too, Michael.' A pause.

'Yes Dad?'

'Your mother's pregnant. Three months. You're going to have a baby brother or sister.'

'At last! Yes! Oh Dad, great! If it's a boy, can we call him Ringo?' I bounced in my seat with happiness.

'I doubt your mother would approve of Ringo,' said Dad 'but one of the other Beatles, names perhaps. Paul. What do you think?' Dad was smiling broadly; stuck in the traffic behind the over-smoking exhaust of an old Austin Seven.

'Oh damn this,' he said, indicating left and turning out of the traffic, away from the direction of the supermarket, 'let's go and see some real butterflies. I've got my net in the car; how do you fancy going to Bude?'

'Ooooh! Bude! Can we have lunch in a café? Will we be able to go on the beach too?'

'I expect so!' said Dad, smiling. 'Hey, we're going somewhere special together, and about time too, son. Perhaps your mother will be in a better mood when we get back.'

'Or a worse one. She likes Bude, Dad.' He went quiet for a moment.

'Then we must tell her what a terrible time we had!

187

Traffic jams! Nowhere to park. The tide in too far, wasps, and Mods and Rockers fighting all over the place.'

'Mods and Rockers only fight on bank holidays, don't they? And do they have them in Bude?'

'They have the worst ones in Bude!' Dad laughed. 'Especially on a Saturday. Hundreds of really mean, ugly ones who stand across the road ready to fight each other, like the goodies and the baddies in *High Noon*.'

'What; really Dad?'

He laughed crazily, and I smiled, resigning to the fact that the joke was now, me.

'What; really?' he mimicked, tears beginning to roll from his eyes. 'Honestly son! Can't you tell when I'm pulling your leg?'

Bude is a small, unspoiled seaside town on the North Cornwall coast. Only forty minutes drive from where we lived, it was a popular destination for day trips, as it had, as we would all say, *everything*. The main beach is a wide, flat bay with a far away, low tide line. It has a small town, rising up on the east side of its cliffs, with hotels and a golf course. On the far west side of the bay is a very small tidal harbour, that meets both the mouth of a wide but shallow river, and the steep-sided, deep Bude Canal. Elegant walkways escort the waterways, and small gardens with bright floral badges brightened the route. It was possible, in those years, to walk all around the place and observe the unusual conventions of other people's business, and so we always did. To the west of the harbour, rising atop the cliffs once more, is a path that traces itself, eventually, along the entire North Cornwall coastline. Apart from some nearby streets and old workers' cottages at the bottom, a path wends its way up and up, through an area of grassy scrub that is especially kept for the conservation of butterflies. Dad especially loved it there, and no trip to Bude was completed without a climb to the top and some time out with the butterfly net. We got to the coast, on this occasion, at lunchtime and ate seaside food; a hot dog and milkshake in a café. Dad put money in the jukebox, and I chose 'Yellow Submarine' and 'Lucy In The Sky.' Dad tried to whistle the tunes, which was embarrassing. We paid and left, and walked the fifty yards through town to the sand. We passed a betting shop, and I saw Dad looking in and then at me, and then at the opening door again, but we just walked on past. Dad went quiet. There were a few hundred people on the beach, and like us, all with their sweaters or jackets on. A westerly wind blew constantly, moderate, but capable of raising the goose-pimples on our arms; but the big, fluffy clouds blew across the horizon and not in from it, and it felt like the first proper day of summer. A fast yellow kite flirted athletically with the sky; a civilization of disparate sandcastles was springing up. We headed straight for the waves of the far tide coming slowly in. With trouser legs rolled up, I ran in the flat, shallow water, kicking small ribbons of foam at Dad, who stood on the dry shore holding our socks and shoes. I walked towards him, kicking arcs of glinting water and shouting names for the new baby.

'Ethelred!'

'NO!' laughed Dad.

'Mungo!'

'Ugh!'

'Belladonna! Cinderella! Hare Krishna!'

The tide and I chased him. He walked backwards to avoid getting his feet unnecessarily wet – we had brought no towel with us. Suddenly, a little wave rushed forward quickly and Dad, leaping back, bumped into a couple and their two children, both boys, a little younger than me.

'I'm so sorry. Terribly sorry, madam, let me help you.' Dad bent down to pick up the buckets and spades he had knocked out of the woman's hands. No other damage was done. The man and woman, at first a little shocked, scowled at him.

'Bloody Paki,' said the woman. 'Bloody get back to where you came from.'

'Yeah, bloody Paki, Enoch's right. Get back . . .' started the man, who looked a bit like a Rocker, I thought fearfully; definitely not a Mod.

'I'm Indian. I'm not from Pakistan, I'm from India.' The Rocker stepped forwards and posed like John Wayne. Oh no. Oh no, please. I looked across to the other boys, who looked as scared as I felt.

'Leave it, Steve. Another time. We're here for the kids.' The woman spoke in tighter tones than she had before; my Dad is six feet tall, and slim but strong. Steve the Rocker squinted as his wife repeated herself, then stepped back.

'Bloody Pakis.'

'I told you. I'm Indian – that is, from INDIA.' Dad's courage rose as the family turned their backs and walked away. 'And I have a degree from your bloody British University in *entomology*.' Dad's voice trailed off as the family walked away. I came out of the sea, which was now lapping round Dad's feet too.

'I bet,' said Dad, 'that they don't even know what bloody entomology is.'

'*Bloody* entomology?' I asked. Dad hit me sharply and painfully round the ear.

'Don't swear,' he said.

* * *

The conservation ground was a wide, open space curving around the ascending cliff. Three mulberry bushes marked the turn-off of the tourist path into the area; and although the nearby tourist-information kiosk showed it on the map, it was not even sign-posted. I knew many of the plants here by name, as they were all the specific foods of insects, particularly butterflies, which I had had to learn about in the past. I greeted them in my mind like old friends and acquaintances, sometimes even muttering their names aloud. Amongst tight little tussocks of different native grasses, bramble and gorse hedges, buddleia, foxgloves, yarrow, thrift and fumitory and many others all nodded their heads in reply. The nearby beach seemed far away, and the air was warmer up on top. We bared our arms to the sun, and looked out at the dancing silver patterns of sunlight dazzling on the water, and the distant haze around Lundy Island. Several small yachts and a larger ketch cut through the sparkling sea, little white waves parting before them and licking the hulls like hungry white hounds before diving back under the blue. Soon enough, Dad was distracted.

'Red admiral, male' he said, pointing with the net in his hand. 'Tortoiseshells, male and female. Come on, let's see who finds the rarest one today.' And he set off on one of the little narrow paths, higher up the cliff.

Everything in the outdoors had come on early that year; a February of blue skies and early magnolias; occasional sunny days in a daffodil March and the driest April for twenty years. On this warm day, dreaming pupae had been stirred from their slumber by the daylight, and the call of freedom beckoned new wings. They edged themselves, crumpled and awkward from the brittle shells of their yesterdays until they were fully reborn to the warm rising air. Red admirals, tortoiseshells, brimstone, cabbage whites, orange tips and more, all performed dainty aerobatics.

'Dad! A comma! I found a comma!'

'Where?' he said, frowning but excited, coming over to me, 'male or female?'

'Male, of course. Look.'

'Hmm. Well done. Certainly rare for this time of year. I'm trying to identify some blues. They won't keep still of course; trying to elude me they are. You try and see. Look. Here's the book.' I didn't really want to look at the book, but did as I was told. The worn-out Collins *Pocket Guide to Butterflies* was put into my hands, and I found the pages for blues and attended to Dad. I looked around for one that had settled, but my eye caught something else. I blinked, to make sure I was really seeing it; ran the name through my mind just to make sure. I looked down at the lower flowers of the just-open, pink foxglove.

'A monarch,' I said softly.

'Of course it's not a bloody monarch,' said Dad, 'it's bloody blue. Come on boy, look over the page . . .' Dad noticed I was paying no attention to him but was looking somewhere else.

'Dad. Look. A monarch. There . . .'

'I don't believe it. I don't bloody believe it. Do you know about the monarch, Michael?' Dad was panting with excitement.

'Yes Dad. It must have . . .'

'. . . come all the way from America or Mexico. They're not native to this country.' He stood suddenly upright and looked with glassy eyes across the Atlantic. He looked back at the monarch again.

'They come here on occasional warm, high winds from

across the ocean, on their journey from Mexico up to California or Oregon, or even Canada in the early summer, just so they can mate and lay their eggs. Then they return all the way to Mexico in the autumn, to die there.'

'Yes Dad. I read about them. They're the symbol for their festival, the Mexican Day of the Dead. The Mexicans say they are people's souls, reborn as butterflies.'

We stared; trying even not to blink. The monarch ceased the opening and closing of its wings, lifted itself off the low flower and rose, it seemed, on the same current of breath that we both suddenly gasped. Entranced by the fold and wave of its yellow-gold wings, our hearts beat uncertainly as it took off into the air just above our heads, moved along with the breeze a little downhill. We ran, stumbling, after it. It descended suddenly, on to a gorse branch, and as it did so, Dad and I began to breathe again.

'For all the wonderful butterflies I have ever seen; ones with the colours of emeralds and sapphires, the ones that fall like flowers from tall jungle trees and feign death, then fly on when a predator has passed; huge, day-flying moths and moon moths that glow in that light – all miraculous – but nowhere near as much as this butterfly that can cross a continent from east to west, north to south, and the ocean, on currents of air, and land here, on wings as fine as . . . as fine as . . .' he was momentarily lost for words '. . . as fine as chance.'

'It is a monarch, isn't it Dad? I mean, it's the king of the butterflies.'

'It is that, Michael. It is the king.'

We watched the butterfly in silence, like two attending devotees upon a great leader. We watched the slow rhythm of its sun-basking, rehearsed flight with the tease of its wings, and held our breath with every lift it took into the air, as if this moment's rare sight of such awe and beauty might be our last. It would then find somewhere to settle, to sup from a flower with its smooth, coiled proboscis, sunbathe, and move on again. About two hours later, when the tide came in fully, and the sea winds rose, we watched our monarch skitter over the edge of the cliff, fly a little out towards the sea and then turn with the wind out across the harbour. It disappeared as if into thin air. Dad spoke softly, slowly. His encounter with the rare and beautiful itinerant had touched him deeply; he was filled with gentle calm.

'Come on Michael. It's time to go.' We walked down the path through the scrub; red admirals still bathed in the sun, tortoiseshells still flitted, blues chased fast amongst the browns and whites, but they were all merely distractions now. Dad kept looking out to sea.

'I'd love to go there, Michael. I'd love to go to America to see some more, some day.'

'We might see some more if we keep coming to Bude too, Dad.'

'That's true, Michael. We certainly might. Let's go and tell your mother about our day; we can't keep secrets from her really. Not any more.'

I am sitting now, on the rug with Emily and James, in the middle of a field, somewhere in California. The sun is low in the sky; out here, sunsets seem to happen faster. Emily and James whisper something to each other from time to time; all I hear is:

'No . . . that way . . . ten minutes to half an hour maybe . . . do you think?' and other such things that imply their anticipation.

I suspect, as it is not difficult to do, that they are planning to show me a monarch butterfly; in some special place they came with Dad. It makes sense, doesn't it? Up here in these hills, no doubt near to mulberry trees, and at this time of the year, it is a certain bet that we can get close to monarchs. I keep my suspicions to myself; I appreciate, with all my heart, that Emily and James are honouring Dad's request. I can feel their excitement, a little anxiety. How losing one's sight increases the other senses!

Emily gasps, and jumps up; we are all getting to our feet again.

'Michael. We're taking the blindfold off now. When your eyes adjust to the light, I want you to focus on the trees. Okay?' and she pulls at the knot on the tied scarf.

'Okay!' and I am blinded; the world is a dazzling swirl of pain in my eyes and I close them. The light diffuses red through my eyelids. I peep a little. Blurred but not so dazzled, I can make out the trees, about thirty feet away. Little old chestnut, some mulberry maybe, some . . . there is some strange blossom on the trees . . . descending from the sky like a phenomenon I cannot make out . . . oh! Oh my dear God! There are butterflies falling from the sky and upon the trees like strange, living snow; like a flittering sky-fall of living beauty. They are monarchs. They are all monarchs! This is unbelievable. Is this happening? There are more and more falling from the tops of the trees and on to the grass. I turn to look at Emily and James, and one is landing on the wrist of Emily's outstretched arm, on her breast like a miraculous brooch; James has one on his hair. I reach out my hand and catch one passing, and it rests there. A miracle! I walk closer to the trees on legs I cannot feel, and drop on to my knees and begin to weep; I gasp the tears deep from my belly and resent them burning, blurring this vision from my eyes. I wipe the tears away, and each breath I breathe fills me with a rush of swirling emotions, as it is the air that has been brushed with the wings of a thousand monarchs.

'They come here this time every year,' says Emily, gently 'and last year we came here with Dad.' I turn and look at her, still on my knees, tears still flowing freely, butterflies settling, ascending, settling again on the ground before me, opening and closing their lacy golden wings, on my outstretched arms and astonished head. 'When Mum was alive, they once came here both together; it was their first visit, just after I became engaged to James. James took us all out here, and showed us.'

'I came here every year with my own parents since I was a kid. It's like the monarchs roost sometimes, just like birds; I've never found out why they do it. Who knows – perhaps they've been having their butterfly rites here in these hills since the beginning of creation. It's all a mystery. A wonderful mystery.'

'You can empty the ashes whenever,' says Emily. 'I thought the breeze would take them like butterfly wings. Oh Daddy. Our very own monarch.' Tears come to her too.

'Dad said he wanted me to scatter his ashes, and that you would show me where,' I say, 'but I had no idea . . . no idea . . .' Words fail. Sometimes it is just better to breathe, and feel, and remember and look forward all at the same time.

So I stand here now, with the people I most love, in the middle of a myriad of swirling miracles. The sun is weighty with red and begins to sink; shadows lengthen and wings begin to settle. Emptying the fragile remains of our father, a first gust of autumn nights kicks up. I pour. Earth to earth, ashes to ashes, dust to dust; as the soul of a foreign butterfly king flits skyward.

LIZ JENSEN

The Girl Who Reversed Progress

SUNDAY 3RD MAY

It's a cheap, no-frills little nightmare, depressingly easy to analyse.

I, Lars Holstein, am in charge of a ship that is sinking slowly into the Baltic. My passengers and crew have bailed out in lifeboats, leaving me alone at the helm in a state of bottomless despair.

– I will go down with my noble vessel! I cry defiantly. But my voice is lost to the rushing waves.

I awake sweating. I've fallen asleep in the Decision Room, my head resting on a pile of petitions demanding mercy for Kristina Smitt, whose execution is due tomorrow.

Kristina Smitt, aged eleven, ideologue, stirrer, rebel, criminal, and founder of the absurd 'Return to Democracy' campaign. Return to Kindergarten, more like. One outcome of this debacle is that I'm having Ritalin put in the water supply at the first opportunity. Medical reports show that like most kids, Kristina Smitt was prescribed it for Attention Deficit Disorder – but she failed to medicate. Just look at how it snowballed.

Her Humane Reckoning's at eleven in the morning. I have a bottle of champagne ready.

Monday 4th May

Repellent news. It is a dark, dark day for the Homeland. Kristina Smitt has escaped, on the very morning of her appointment with justice. It turns out she sweet-talked the governor of the Facility. Hooked him with her cute Daddy's Girl act, then reeled him in with some tear-jerking hogwash about freedom, equality, you don't want to see a little girl die do you, blah blah blah. So what does he do but cave in, and sneak the kid out of the Facility in his own BMW, setting her loose somewhere on the coast with a stash of money, a Kalashnikov, and a fatherly kiss on the cheek.

All around me, people are going insane.

This morning, my Cabinet and I talk for an hour in the Decision Room, updating our strategy. I try to put a brave face on things but when the others have left, I put my head in my hands and silently scream. The Kristina Smitt crisis – the most humiliating episode in my political career – has now reached grotesque proportions. 'Grotesque' is not a word I would normally use. Nor, for that matter, is 'humiliation'. But my vocabulary has ventured into a new realm of late. My wife reports that ever since the kid began her campaign of social disruption last year, I have been cursing aloud in my sleep, like someone with nocturnal Tourette's Syndrome. My looks have altered too. I used to appear so suave. Now, the newspaper photos show the nation's leader as a scared puppet, pop-eyed with exhaustion. I would cross the street to avoid myself, not even waiting for the Little Green Man.

Kristina Smitt, by contrast, looks like a pretty china doll. Imagine a whole nation brought to its knees by a single, pre-pubescent female! And then imagine what it is like to be Lars Holstein, the man in charge! I feel as powerless as a worm.

Tuesday 5th May

Prophetic, that I should have dreamed of a ship, because the little minx's latest stunt is to hijack a Norwegian cruise liner full of affluent members of the Third Age. She held passengers and crew in the *Global Pleasure*'s concert hall and subjected them to an hour of evangelistic bullshit about freedom and human rights and the immorality of Humane Disposal, then issued a smooth ultimatum: stay on board 'for an educational experience', or 'jump into a lifeboat and take your chances'.

When I learned how many opted to stay on board for the 'educational experience', I threw my cup of coffee at the wall. – What's the matter with people? I yelled. – Can't they see she's just a silly little attention-seeker?

– You're taking it all very personally, Boss, murmured my Chief of Staff, Hans Winkel. For the last year, Hans and I have had one sole topic of discussion: the latest twist in Miss Smitt's grandiose psychodrama. Gone are our pleasurable musings on how much other nations envy us, our nonchalant discussions about razor wire and welfare fraud, economic security and the new vertical pig farms.

– Of course I take it personally! I snapped. – To tell you the truth, Hans, were it not for my belief in the rule of law, I'd pack it all in and drive down to the south of France. I'd be happy to make a humble living selling those Mediterranean fish – what are they called, *bouillabaisse*? – in the market. Chew raw garlic, and forget I was ever the elected leader of the most socially advanced nation in the northern hemisphere.

– *Bouillabaisse* is a soup, not a fish, he corrected me. – Try *dorade*.

Hans is the most unbearably pedantic man I have ever met, and at that point I did not hesitate to tell him so. I also told him he could leave the Decision Room pronto, and not return until he had some good news to tell me about the noxious child. That was five hours ago. I haven't seen him since. My blood pressure is up. I check it hourly with a little gizmo.

An e-mail update from Kim Dogger, head of Security. The *Global Pleasure*, still under Kristina Smitt's control, has made a series of lightning recruitment visits to Violent Man Island, Violent Woman Island, Sociopath Island, Tax Criminal Island and Manic Depressive Island. Loaded with thousands of enthusiastic new passengers, who cannot believe their luck at being freed, the ship is now headed for Muslim Island. One can only imagine what a dangerous conflux of humanity already seethes below the decks of the *Global Pleasure*; now, terrifyingly, the followers of Mohammed are to be added to the mix. I phone my ageing mother to warn her of the increasing danger.

– Don't listen to those rebel broadcasts, Mother. The kid's opening up the islands, de-quarantining the misfits. It's a can of worms. Every nutcase and crook and foreigner in the Homeland's on the loose now. Keep your doors and windows locked, and only answer the red phone. The red phone is the one she and I speak on. Like the blood pressure gizmo, it's one of the perks of my job.

– But Lars, dear, Kristina Smitt is so charming, she says, her old woman's voice high and frail. – And what a grownup head she has on her young shoulders! What she's saying reminds me of the old days. You know, before you put all the bad people on the islands, dear. Your re-what's-it thing.

– *Re-structuring*! I shouted. It's called *re-structuring*!

– Calm down dear. All I'm saying is it reminds me of –

– But that's exactly why she's so *dangerous*, Mother! I

could slap her for her stupidity. – Do you realise she wants us to remove all the social quarantine mechanisms, and go back to the dark ages of unfettered immigration and law-lessness? That *she wants losers to have the vote*?

– I would have loved a little girl like her, my foolish old mother continues, oblivious. – With those gorgeous blonde curls. But she's more than just a pretty face, isn't she? All that passionate talk about freedom and dignity for all . . . you can't fake passion, can you? It brings tears to your eyes.

Is she trying to goad me? Isn't it enough for her that her only child is Prime Minister? (*You can't fake passion.* What's she talking about? I have made a pretty decent career of it!) Furious, I slam down the phone. You nurture a society, keep it pure and simple and clean-edged, a shining city on a hill, an example to the world. And then you watch one bad apple do its work, even infecting your own mother. Lord above, how fragile it all is.

Next came a depressing phone call from my steely Interior Minister, Vera Gunk: it appears that 'the Enemy' as Vera calls her, has launched an Internet recruitment drive, electronically summoning as many as half a million more followers to her cause, with figures rising by the hour.

– She's targeting the weakest members of society, of course, spat Vera. – Kiddies like herself, and the Alzheimer's Brigade.

I sighed and confessed that even my own mother seemed to be in the kid's demonic thrall.

– Join the club, she said bitterly. – My father's actually talking of signing up. I told him if he did, he could forget about having a daughter.

– What did he say to that?

There was a pause. I sensed pain on the other end of the line.

– He said he'd think about it.

My wife Bettina deals with our seven children more than I do, as I am a busy man. But I have a good relationship with them, I think. The photo opportunities always show us smiling and looking like a contented family, at ease with itself. On impulse, I ring Bettina and ask her to send me our fifth child, twelve-year-old Fritz.

– Tell me son, I say as he stands gawkily in front of my big desk. – What do you make of the Smitt kid?

– Do you want me to say what you want to hear, Dad, or shall I tell you what I really think? he asks. He looks innocent enough, but I'm not sure I like his tone.

I hesitate, torn. – What you really think, I say eventually. – That's what I always want you to tell me, Fritz.

– No it isn't, he replies defiantly. But I decide to overlook his insolence, for now. I need his feedback here. I can punish him later. I reach for my blood pressure gizmo and strap it on to my arm, then nod for Fritz to continue. – I think she's cool, he says.

– Cool? Cool, as in? I can't keep the rage out of my voice.

– Cool, as in, she thinks it's unfair for people who don't have blond hair to be put on special islands. And people who aren't Christians. And mad people. And criminals, and all that stuff. She thinks everyone's equal, and everyone deserves an equal right to –

But Fritz gets no further. My gizmo, which has been climbing the scale, begins to beep loudly.

– Just get out of here! I snap. – Before you give me a heart attack! As Fritz scurries out, I gulp down a Valium.

My pulse back to normal, I watch Vera's broadcast. Her face is caught in an expression of permanent grumpiness which excites me. I find myself admiring the ever-impressive

Ms Gunk more and more. I have even allowed myself to imagine what it might be like to be whipped by her. I picture her controlled features flashing with sudden ecstasy as she lashes rhythmically.

Wednesday 7th May.
Yesterday I was in despair; today I am angry. I shouted at Hans Winkel this morning, yelled till I was hoarse. I smashed my fist on the table, badly hurting my knuckles in the process, and told him he was a moron, and what sort of administrative system did he think he was running, if it couldn't outwit one rogue female? He gave me a long, steady look.

– How long is it since you left this building, Boss? I don't think you've been out on the streets among the people in . . . well it must be months, mustn't it?

– A captain always stays at the helm of his ship, I snapped. – Are you criticising my style of leadership?

– Not at all, he said. But I didn't like his smile – Have you seen the opinion polls? He went on. – A lot of people think she's talking sense. They like her manifesto. They reckon it's 'very civilised.' She's got charisma. You can't argue with charisma.

– Oh can't you? I shouted. – Well I bloody well can!

There was a painful silence. – Will that be all, Prime Minister? he said eventually. In that moment, I suddenly wondered if Kristina Smitt's message might actually be working on him, too. Paranoid, I know. But it's what I felt.

Desperate for some loyalty, I phoned Vera Gunk. Gratifyingly, she expressed disdain at Hans' lack of moral fibre. But she finished with a warning.

– Keep your dignity, Prime Minister. – Or people will think less of you.

Later I lay awake next to my sleeping wife, thinking about the excitingly stern tone Vera Gunk has begun to use with me.

Handcuffs, maybe?

Thursday 8th May
The Homeland is not used to appealing to the outside world for help, but I am now desperate enough to be writing to the President of Britain. His nation, being an island, will surely understand the plight of the Homeland. And take a nervous interest in it, given the geographical proximity.

Dear Sir, You will know us to be a moral people, rightly proud of the radical social reforms we have implemented in the last decade. But now, humbled by our current crisis, we beg you to share the burden of our nightmare – which may, sooner than you think, become your nightmare too.

You are aware of our recent history, as a nation. The Homeland's ground-breaking policy of deploying outlying islands for social quarantine purposes will be familiar to you. Thanks to initiatives taken in the Homeland, islandisation is now a system which is recognised, admired and copied globally. You will also know that when it comes to individuals deemed a threat to national stability, we apply a strict Humane Reckoning policy. Such stern measures, however, demand the consent of a mentally stable citizenship. The Ritalin initiative, begun twenty years ago, has proved effective. But it is not foolproof – as the case of Kristina Smitt testifies so tragically. We are now paying a heavy price for this oversight, in the form of a threatened revolution led by one powerful child misfit.

You, sir, have shown nerve in times of crisis. I believe the hijacked ship is headed for your waters. You have sophisticated weaponry, capable of targeting and sinking such a vessel. We urge you to use it. We can supply the co-ordinates. I beg you not to hesitate.

Yours sincerely, Lars Holstein.

Then, just as I am printing out my missive, Hans enters.

– Unexpected news, sir.

– I told you not to contact me if it wasn't good news. So is it good news?

– It depends on how you look at it, sir, he said shiftily.

– So how do you look at it?

– I think it's good, sir, he said. – That's why I came. But you may not agree.

– Well what is it then?

– She wants a meeting.

– With me?

– Who else? You're the boss, Boss. One-to-one.

My heart began to beat frantically. An uncharacteristic attack of cowardice overcame me, and I confess that for a brief moment, I felt like vomiting.

– I thought she was heading for Britain.

– Wishful thinking on your part I fear, Boss, he smirked.

– Fine, I snapped, crumpling my letter to the British Prime minister and hurling it in the bin. – But I need another briefing first. Get me Vera Gunk.

– No need. A team of shrinks is on its way. They'll tell you how to deal with her. Remember, she's just a kid.

And he gave a smile which I did not very much like the look of.

Five minutes later, a knock at the door.

– She's here, sir, whispered Hans. – Unexpectedly early. He looked scared, thrilled. A little in love.

– But the team of shrinks! Vera! Where are they?

– No time sir, he whispered. – Just listen to the kid, Boss. You can handle it. I've ordered her a Coca-Cola.

He closed the door, but not before I had smelled the whiff of high-level betrayal.

She fixed me with her clear, clean eyes. Doll's eyes, like glass. She was chewing gum.

– It's over, Uncle Lars, she said. Despite the seriousness of her tone, her voice was absurdly babyish. – You can go home to your family. I'll be taking care of things from now on.

– What will you do?

– What I said I would in my manifesto, she said innocently. – You know. Free the islands. Give everyone the vote. Make it how it was when my granny was young.

– Destroy all we've built? Destabilise the whole nation? *Reverse progress*?

– Who said it was progress? Do you really think that just because time moves on, everything gets better? That's a bit crazy, Uncle Lars. A bit bo-bo.

And she blew a bubble. I watched as it punctured and collapsed, unleashing a little gust of sweetness into the Decision Room.

– We're the envy of the world, I stammered. – Other countries look to us for guidance. We're the future. She gave me a sweet, forgiving smile. – Come out onto the balcony, Uncle Lars, she said gently. – And give the citizens a last wave.

The fresh air hit me like a punch. How long was it since I had ventured outdoors? I couldn't remember. I looked down at the scene below me and gasped. A horde of filthy-looking, unwashed people swarmed all over the flowerbeds, popping open cans of fizzy drinks, eating popcorn and dropping litter. Vile pop music blared from a ghetto-blaster. I saw old men in wheelchairs, children with unbrushed hair, muslims in their traditional garb, and some hard-faced men and women with tattoos whom I guessed to be criminals from the Violent Islands. On my lawn! My beautiful Prime Ministerial lawn!

Next thing I knew, Kristina Smitt was standing on a chair next to me, a megaphone at her lips.

– Friends! The music faded and the crowd let loose a raucous cheer. – Uncle Lars has decided to step down!

More cheering. – Wave, Uncle Lars, she murmured to me. – Just wave and nod. No-one's going to shoot you.

But it was death nevertheless. I don't know how long I stood on the balcony inhaling the fresh air I had been deprived of for so long, and feeling the hatred of my people. Minutes? Hours? As the cheering finally disintegrated into a white noise of whistles and jeers, my eye alighted on my son Fritz. He looked up at me and gave me the thumbs up.

I was led away by a female dwarf and a man who appeared to be blind. In the corridor, in the midst of the confusion, I spotted my trusty Vera. For a moment, my heart lifted – until she pointed at me accusingly, her face contorted with loathing.

– I always hated him! she yelled. – I was on your side all the time, my dear Kristina! I never wanted you executed!

Kristina gave her a long, hard look, then blew an enormous pink bubble right in Vera's face. When it burst, a sweet breath of cerise filled the corridor. Vera had her answer.

* * *

And so I am a citizen again. An ordinary man living with my wife and children in a flat in the midst of the haphazard, lawless community they call the 'today's society'. A few middle-aged people like me still obey the Little Green Man and all he stands for, still eat roast pork on a Sunday, still mistrust the Euro, still think that there's too much human litter on the streets. But we are a dying breed.

Author Biographies

NAOMI ALDERMAN was born in London in 1974. She has a BA in philosophy, politics and economics from Oxford University and has recently completed the MA in creative writing at the University of East Anglia, where she was the winner of the David Higham Award.

VICTORIA BRIGGS is thirty-two years old. She works for the *Guardian* and is a part-time student on the MA writing (prose fiction) programme at Middlesex University.

LESLEY GLAISTER teaches a Master's degree in writing at Sheffield Hallam University and lives between Sheffield and Orkney. She is the author of nine novels, including the award-winning *Honour thy Father*. Her latest novel is *As Far As You Can Go*.

CAREY JANE HARDY took a break in nursing to do a degree in English Literature and has since worked as a college lecturer in health studies and creative writing. She was a winner of the Ian St James Award, short-listed in a novel competition run by Writer's Forum, and her play *Let It Be Me*, is to be published by Samuel French. She lives in Worcestershire.

LIZ JENSEN is the author of *The Paper Eater*, *Egg Dancing* and *Ark Baby* which was short-listed for the *Guardian* Fiction Prize. She has worked as a journalist, radio producer and sculptor and now lives in London. Her most recent novels are *War Crimes for the Home*, about wartime brides and American GIs, and *The Ninth Life of Louis Drax*.

LUCY LEPCHANI is 41 and has recently returned to writing after many years of bringing up children, community arts work and various other 'proper jobs.' She lives in Devon with her partner Sean, and has four children – three of whom have finally left home!

MORAG MACINNES was born and lives in Orkney. She is a freelance arts worker and WEA tutor, interested in oral reminiscence. She has taught creative writing, written and directed community plays, edited community anthologies and had stories published in Scotland.

JANE MALTBY divides her time between looking after her two sons, running a business promoting Yorkshire food, occasional journalism and writing fiction. She lives in Leeds and is married to a solicitor.

MORAG McDOWELL was born in Glasgow and started writing short stories after leaving university. She has won various prizes including the Macallan/*Scotland on Sunday* awards and has been published in magazines and anthologies. She works in adult education and writes as much as she can.

RACHAEL McGILL was born in the Shetland Islands in 1974 and now lives in East London. She has had a number of plays performed and translates theatre from French and German. Her story *A Tasmanian Tiger in London* was published in the Macallan/*Scotland on Sunday* short story collection 2002. She is working on plays and stories and pretending to write a novel.

HANNAH MURGATROYD is 26 and has been writing for as long as she can remember. She is also studying for an MA in illustration at the Royal College of Art. She enjoys writing short fiction and most of her stories are set in America, which she visits as often as she can afford.

MAGGIE O'FARRELL was born in Northern Ireland in 1972 and grew up in Wales and Scotland. She has worked as a waitress and chambermaid, arts administrator and journalist. She is the author of *After You'd Gone* and *My Lover's Lover*. She lives in London.

HILARY PLEWS was born in North Yorkshire and grew up in various army camps around the world. She studied English literature at university, before spending 22 years as a solicitor, specialising in immigration and asylum law. She completed an MA in creative writing at Middlesex University and works with refugees through the public library service. A short story was short listed for the London New Writing competition and she is working on a novel set in Swaledale and Hackney.

KATE PULLINGER is a novelist whose books include *Weird Sister* and *The Last Time I Saw Jane*, and the story collection *My Life as a Girl in a Men's Prison*. She also writes for the web. Visit her website at www.katepullinger.com

LISA SABBAGE was born in New Zealand and moved to London in 1993, working as a journalist. She began writing short fiction and has had stories published in two anthologies and on BBC London Radio. She is working on her first novel.

KAMILA SHAMSIE was born in 1973 in Pakistan and received the Award for Literature in Pakistan in 1999. Her first novel *In the City by the Sea* was short-listed for the John Llewellyn Rhys/*Mail on Sunday* prize and her second, *Salt and Saffron*, won her a place on Orange's list of '21 writers for the 21st century.' *Kartography* was published in 2002. She lives in London and Karachi.

FRANCINE STOCK is a writer and broadcaster who worked for the BBC's *Newsnight* from 1988 to 1993. She currently presents Radio 4's nightly arts programme *Front Row*. Her first novel, *A Foreign Country*, was short-listed for the Whitbread First Novel Award in 1999 and her most recent novel is *Man-Made Fibre*. She lives in London with her husband and two daughters.

VALERIE THORNTON has received a Scottish Arts Council Writer's Bursary, been short-listed for the Macallan/*Scotland on Sunday* Short Story Prize and her creative writing textbook *Working Words* won joint first prize as *Times Educational Supplement Scotland* and Saltire Society Scottish Educational Book of the Year. Her first collection of poems, *Catacoustics*, was published in 2000. She has worked as a creative writing tutor for twenty years and was Royal Literary Fund Writing Fellow at Glasgow University from 2001–2003 and is now an RLF Project Fellow, helping teachers in training and in service to develop both their own and their pupils' creative writing skills.

ERICA WAGNER, literary editor of *The Times*, is the author of *Gravity: Stories* (Granta) and *Ariel's Gift: Ted Hughes, Sylvia Plath and the Story of Birthday Letters* (Faber and Faber). She has judged the Man Booker, Whitbread, Forward and Orange Prizes. Her stories have been widely published and broadcast and she was one of the first winners of the Asham Award in 1996. She lives in London.

A NOTE ON THE TYPE

The text of this book is set in Linotype Sabon, named after the type founder, Jacques Sabon. It was designed by Jan Tschichold and jointly developed by Linotype, Monotype and Stempel, in response to a need for a typeface to be available in identical form for mechanical hot metal composition and hand composition using foundry type.

Tschichold based his design for Sabon roman on a fount engraved by Garamond, and Sabon italic on a fount by Granjon. It was first used in 1966 and has proved an enduring modern classic.